Contents

**Biddy Baxter
Edward Barnes
& Rosemary Gill
devised and
wrote The
Blue Peter Book.**

55p

Hello There!

And welcome to our Eighth Blue Peter Book! So much has happened since book number Seven it's difficult to know where to begin–things like Princess Anne visiting the studio to show her souvenirs of our Blue Peter Royal Safari–two members of the crew of our Inshore Rescue Boat, Blue Peter 1, flying to East Pakistan to help the victims of the terrible cyclone and floods, and our special award from the Royal National Lifeboat Institution.

Talking of awards reminds us that we won two more last year–and two *this* year. The first was from the Society of Film and Television Arts–a group of

Do you recognise any of these photographs? They've all been in Blue Peter. Turn to the end for the answers

2

3

5

1

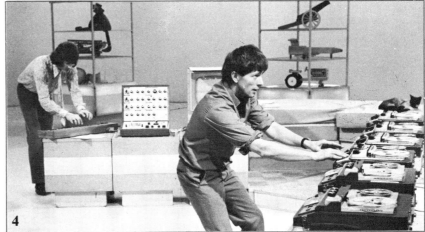

4

experts who pick out the best programmes each year. The second was from the *Sun* newspaper, whose readers voted us the Top Children's Programme. It's a big compliment to be voted for like this–so you can imagine how thrilled we were to be voted "Top" two years in succession–because we won the *Sun* TV award in 1971 as well. And the fourth was a Silver Heart awarded to us by the Variety Club of Great Britain who said Blue Peter was The Greatest Children's Programme. We're very proud of all our awards and we've given them a special place of honour in the Blue Peter office.

Our saddest blow has undoubtedly been the death of dear old Patch. He caught a very rare disease known as E coli septicaemia and in spite of the best possible treatment, nothing could save him. We still miss him dreadfully, but at least he wasn't in pain when he died. Later on we hope to have a new puppy on the programme–but we'll always remember Patch as a faithful friend, and one of the best dogs in the world.

We've broken several records since our last book. Not only the ones mentioned in the new Guinness Book of Records, but by receiving 108,000 entries for our Train of the Future Competition–more than for any other competition we've ever had. And most important of all–by breaking our target for our Blue Peter Appeal *before* the end of the year, and reaching our second target just one week later. You can read all about our Holiday Caravans and our Log Cabin on page 54. Again, thanks to you, a lot of people are going to be much happier this year. Over three thousand children will be having their first ever holiday because you collected all those spoons and forks.

If you haven't managed to write to us yet–try and send us a letter soon. Nearly all the things we do on Blue Peter are because of your suggestions and ideas. We enjoy hearing about your pets and the adventures you have, too. We'd like to know your favourite things in this book as well, so that we can make our ninth book even better! And here's a reminder of our address–it's quite simple:

Blue Peter
BBC Television Centre
London, W12 7RJ

So when you've read the book and done the competition, and solved the mystery picture and the detective story–why not write to us–we're all looking forward to hearing from you!

Jason   Petra

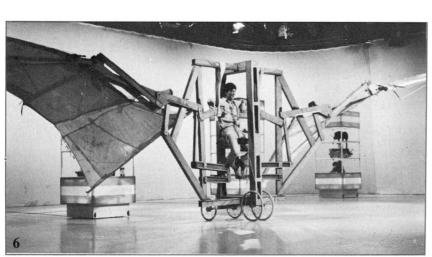

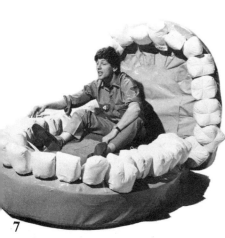

night
on a
bare
mountain

I always look forward to the first fall of snow in the winter. It's true that it's a nuisance on the roads, but it makes even the dreariest landscape look marvellous–and then there's sledging, skating and, if you're lucky, even ski-ing.

But living in the town, you tend to forget that snow has got a sinister side–in fact, snow can be a killer. Every year, literally hundreds of people die from what must be a particularly horrible death–exposure. The great tragedy is that given a few simple tools and a little know-how, many of them would be alive today.

Because on Blue Peter we often have to go off at a moment's notice to cover stories all over the world, and in every sort of weather, I decided

that it would be a good thing if I did a course on snow survival, so one Thursday, straightaway after Blue Peter, I flew off to Scotland to keep an appointment with Bombardier Bruce James of the Army Mountaineering Centre.

After a journey by plane, train, car and ski-lift, I met Bruce on the bleak, exposed side of the highest mountain in the Cairngorms. Mussorgsky once wrote a piece of music called "Night on the Bare Mountain" which might have been our theme tune, because we had no hut, no tent, in fact no form of shelter at all.

It was three hours to nightfall, the temperature was five degrees below freezing and falling rapidly. Twelve degrees of frost is quite common in the Cairngorms at night.

"What's the form?" I asked Bruce.

"Well, if we are going to survive, we've got to dig ourselves a snow-hole," replied Bruce, handing me a spade.

There was about 12 foot of snow on the mountainside so we set to work burrowing away like rabbits. The first thing to do was to make an entrance level with the top of our heads and then tunnel straight into the mountain. The shovels were lightweight, with a sharp cutting edge, and a gadget which dropped the blade at right angles to the handle, turning it into a scraper. But about five feet in, the snow was packed so hard that I could make no impression with the shovel. The light was just beginning to fade, and as I chopped off a few pathetic flakes of snow and ice, I began to feel just a little bit uneasy.

"Hang on, John, I'll get the ice-saw," said Bruce. This was another lightweight tool with huge teeth that went through ice like butter. I was about to fling blocks of it triumphantly down the mountain-side when Bruce said:

"Just a sec.–that's going to be our

7

front door!" The last thing a snow survivor does before turning in for the night is to build up the entrance with solid blocks of snow.

We dug a tunnel about 8 feet long, and then struck off at right angles to hollow out the room which was going to be our home for the night. It was three feet high and about four feet wide, and whilst it wasn't exactly centrally heated, it really felt quite warm and snug inside.

Bruce smoothed off the roof to prevent nasty drops of water dripping down our necks in the night, whilst I dug little shelves into the walls and stuck lighted candles on them. When we'd finished, it looked like one of those trendy underground discothèques!

"All I need now is a nice hot cup of coffee!"

"Then have one," said Bruce, and pulled a jar of coffee and two mess tins out of his rucksack.

"Yeah–but what do we do about water?" I said.

"Just scrape it off the roof, boy," he grinned.

A pan full of snow was soon two steaming cups of coffee. We heard the wind building up outside, but we were warm and secure in our snow-hole. The night on a bare mountain wasn't going to be so bad after all!

Digging a snow hole is tough work, but the ice-saw helped to cut out huge chunks of frozen snow.

We made the entrance just big enough to crawl through.

I scraped a panful of snow off the roof…

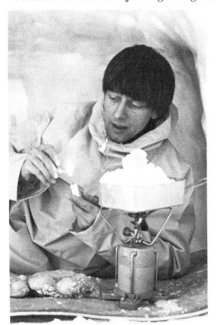

…put it on the portable stove, and five minutes later, Bruce and I were drinking two steaming cups of coffee.

8

Blue Peter Royal Safari

Val says : The most exciting thing this year—at least for me—was the Blue Peter Royal Safari with Princess Anne.

And the most memorable day on the Safari was when we went riding and suddenly came across this African village. All the children rushed out to meet us and they proudly showed off their new litter of puppies.

The African children were extremely interested in the horses, but they had no idea one of the riders was a Royal Princess!

AZTECS

On our Mexican Expedition, we explored the ancient Aztec city of Teotihuacan. Puffing and blowing, we struggled up the steps to the top of the Pyramid of the Sun. It wasn't so much the height that left us gasping, it was the thin mountain air. We had an altitude problem, just like our World Cup football squad when they played in Mexico. All the same, it was fun, and as we stood at the summit, it was hard to believe that hundreds of years ago the very steps that we had climbed had once run red with the blood of human sacrifice. For this ancient pyramid was built by the Aztec Indians. They worshipped strange gods, and over their kingdom ruled their High Priest and Emperor—the Great Montezuma! He ruled supreme until one day the first Mexican Expedition ever approached the gates of his palace.

1 Montezuma was all-powerful. He lived in a palace at Tenochtitlan and he dressed in rich clothes decorated with silver and the feathers of rare birds. The Aztecs thought that Montezuma and his empire would live for ever. But one day

2 spies came to Montezuma with a tale so terrifying that the whole Aztec kingdom felt threatened. The spies drew pictures to show what they had seen.

3 They showed a little band of white-faced men, their bearded leader dressed in black and carrying a strange banner. Though hopelessly outnumbered by the Indians, they were winning every battle and drawing closer and closer to Tenochtitlan.

4 Montezuma looked in an ancient book of prophecies and what he saw amazed him. It said that in this very year, 1519, the man-god Quetzalcoatl would return to earth. He would come as a white-faced man, dressed in black. Was this really Quetzalcoatl? Montezuma daren't attack a god, so he did nothing.

5 But the stranger was not a god. He was Hernan Cortes, a Spaniard, who had come to conquer Mexico and bring the true Christian religion to the Indians. He carried a picture of the Virgin Mary on his banner, and he rode on a horse.

6 The Aztecs had never seen horses before, and to them Hernan Cortes appeared to be a terrifying monster. Worst of all he brought

7 cannons. Hundreds of Indians were blown to bits as they tried to stop the Spaniards, but day by day, Cortes and his handful of men advanced nearer and nearer Montezuma's capital city.

8 At last Cortes reached Tenochtitlan. He stared in amazement. It was richer and more beautiful than any city in Spain. "The battle to win this city will be terrible," thought Cortes. But Montezuma himself came out to greet the strangers.

9 Montezuma treated the Spaniards as honoured guests and loaded them with treasures. The two men became firm friends, until one day, Hernan Cortes asked to see inside one of the temples. Together they climbed slowly up one of the Pyramids.

10 When Cortes reached the top he was disgusted. Inside the temple the walls were red with the blood of human sacrifice. Stinking piles of human bones lay everywhere.

11 "This cruel sacrifice must stop," said Cortes. "The temples must be destroyed, and here we will build a shrine to the Virgin Mary and teach the true Christian religion. Arrest the Emperor Montezuma!"

12 Montezuma was kept prisoner in his own palace. Now he knew that Cortes was *not* the god Quetzalcoatl, but it was too late!

13 Suddenly Montezuma died. Some say he died of despair, some say that a stone thrown by an Indian killed him, and some that Cortes himself ordered him to be strangled. Now, without their leader, the Aztecs were powerless.

14 They rose against the Spanish, but they were no match for them. The Spaniards made the proud Aztecs slaves and took away their treasures and their gold. In no time at all they broke down the beautiful palaces of Tenochtitlan. Montezuma's great city and the whole Aztec Empire were destroyed for ever. But for Cortes, the Expedition to Mexico was a triumph!

RIDE 'EM COWBOY

Everybody thought we were going to fall off. But we didn't. The honour of Blue Peter was at stake—and we weren't going to let it down!

Johnny's horse shot round the ring at a gallop and straight out again! The crowd fell about. They thought it was the funniest thing they'd ever seen. We began to enjoy ourselves. With the laughter and cheers of the crowd ringing in our ears we knew that we would never forget our best day in Mexico— the day we joined the cowboys and rode in the Charreada!

Viva los Ingleses!
Hurrah for the English!

That's what the crowd roared one day in Mexico City as Val, John and I shot into the ring on huge, thoroughbred horses. The dust flew, the horses reared, and the sun blazed down. It was a shattering experience, and one that we'd never expected!

At breakfast one morning, we'd decided to go and see a special Mexican treat called a Charreada. It's like a rodeo—a dazzling display of brilliant horsemanship by some of the best riders in the world—the Charros.

The Charros are the smartest cowboys you could ever see. Their leather suits and huge sombrero hats are covered with beautiful silver decorations, and the splendour of their clothes is equalled only by their skill on horseback. Everybody in Mexico City seemed to have come to the show. We found a seat in the middle of the crowd and settled down to enjoy ourselves. We saw bareback riding, then the lassooing champion of Mexico, spinning and twisting his rope, and jumping in and out of the loop as though it was as easy as falling off a bike. Next came brave men riding bucking broncos and wild steers.

Then suddenly, it was our turn! The crowd had seen the Blue Peter cameras filming. Now they wanted *us* to give them a show!

In no time at all, we'd been given huge sombrero hats and were mounted on enormous snorting horses. It was pretty frightening— especially for Val. She'd been given a gunbelt and a six shooter to wear, and every time she bumped up and down in the saddle she was afraid she was going to shoot herself!

Then the band struck up, the spectators cheered, and we were pelting round the ring.

No 532

Alison Beattie sent us this photograph of the derailed Blue Peter. Her grandad is sitting on the wheel.

The 532 Blue Peter restored in the LNER livery she would have had *before* nationalisation.

The 532 Blue Peter

An important invitation arrived in the Blue Peter office last autumn:

"Dear Val, John and Peter," it said, "You will be pleased to know that work on the Blue Peter Locomotive is now complete. Would you come to Doncaster on 22nd November to perform the Renaming Ceremony for us?

Signed: The Blue Peter Locomotive Society."

We had no second thoughts about accepting. After all, we'd followed the progress of the 532 very closely, ever since she was saved from the scrap-heap in 1968. We hardly dared to believe she'd be restored so quickly—22nd November was certainly going to be a day not to be missed!

Even if you aren't particularly interested in steam-trains, the story of the 532 is an exciting one. She's a Class A-2 Pacific locomotive—this was the new type of loco that went into service in the very last week of the old LNER. After nationalisation, British Railways went ahead with

the LNER plans, and fourteen locomotives were built at the Doncaster Plant Works. They were all named after racehorses, and the eighth—No. 60532—was called Blue Peter after the famous horse that won the Derby in 1939. Blue Peter went into service on 25th March 1948 and carried the green livery of the newly formed British Railways.

Then, one year later, the Blue Peter was sent to Scotland where she stayed in service for 17 years. But in 1966 she was withdrawn and was left out in a siding in the open for two whole years. With no protection from the weather—a target for vandals and souvenir hunters—the Blue Peter was in a very sorry state indeed when she was discovered by two railway enthusiasts, Geoffrey Drury and Brian Hollingsworth. Together, they formed the Blue Peter Locomotive Society, with the aim of restoring the loco to her former glory. And not only that, the plan was to give her the

LNER livery, and the number she would have had *before* nationalisation.

Restoring a hundred and sixty-one tons of rusty scrap iron is quite a task!

We know, because we helped with some of the painting, and made several progress reports. The Blue Peter was allowed to return to the Plant Works at Doncaster where everyone who remembered the old days of steam helped with the repair work. One very skilful craftsman actually came out of retirement to paint some of the delicate line work.

Progress was slow but sure—in spite of several baffling mysteries. For instance, there was the colossal amount of damage *underneath* the locomotive. This couldn't have been done by vandals and no one could explain how it had happened until one day, Alison Beattie sent us a photograph and an amazing letter. Alison said:

"*I thought you would be interested in this picture of the*

At 3.00 p.m. the doors of the locomotive sheds were opened—and with a mighty surge, the crowds broke the rope barriers!

At 3.15 p.m. Val made a very good speech and performed the actual Renaming Ceremony with a bottle of champagne.

After the Ceremony the 532 Blue Peter was open to inspection by the 60,000-strong crowd.

engine Blue Peter. My Grandad is sitting on top, waiting for the repair crane.''
and the photograph showed what looked like a wrecked train with Alison's grandad sitting on an upturned wheel. This photograph gave us the vital clue. Some time during her working life, the Blue Peter had obviously been derailed on an embankment, which explained why her underside was so badly knocked about.

There was another mystery early in 1970 when the loco was being temporarily housed at York. Two of her massive big-end bearing rings were stolen, and the thieves were never discovered. That meant she would be unable to run until they were replaced—which was no easy task. Big-end bearing rings have to be specially made to fit individual engines—the Blue Peter's original plans were missing, so it took many months for new ones to be constructed.

But in spite of the setbacks, the Blue Peter was ready in time for her grand Renaming Ceremony—and 22nd November 1970 was a day we'll never forget!

Even though we arrived very early, thousands and thousands of railway enthusiasts were already converging on Doncaster. British Rail had put on loads of extra trains, and the town was thronging with crowds of people from as far away as Weston-super-Mare, Tunbridge Wells and King's Lynn. Traffic was directed by AA signs saying: BLUE PETER CEREMONY

with an arrow pointing in the right direction for the Locomotive Works, and cars were parked for miles around.

At 2.30 sharp, the York Railway Institute Silver Band struck up with a medley of rousing tunes. Twenty-five minutes later, we struggled towards the Renaming Ceremony Platform—struggled because by this time the crowd had grown to more than 60,000 people! We could scarcely believe our eyes—and neither could the Mayor of Doncaster, Alderman Mrs Olive Sunderland, who was a bit shaky anyway, as it was her first day up after a dose of 'flu. The General Manager of the British Rail Eastern Region, Mr I. A. Campbell, was pretty staggered, too.

At 3.00 p.m., the doors of the locomotive sheds were opened and out rolled the 532 Blue Peter, her brand-new paintwork gleaming in the sun. This was the moment we'd all been waiting for—and for some the excitement of seeing the Blue Peter was too great. With a mighty surge, the crowds broke the rope barrier—the York Railway Institute Silver Band was submerged in a sea of banners and duffle coats—our platform was nearly toppled over, and the loco herself was almost hidden from view. Fortunately no damage was done, and at 3.15 p.m. Val made a very good speech and stepped forward to break a bottle of champagne over the smoke-box door. We pulled two gold silk cords attached to purple velvet curtains and revealed the 532 Blue Peter's shining brass name-plates.

''We take great pleasure in renaming this engine 532 . . .'' Val said, and crunch went the bottle.

''HURRAH'' Yelled the crowd with a cheer that must have echoed as far as Leeds—the 532 Blue Peter was well and truly renamed!

P.S. The next big event in the 532 Blue Peter's history will be getting-up steam. So far, British Rail have been reluctant to let her run on their lines, but the Blue Peter Locomotive Society hasn't given up all hope. Meanwhile, if you'd like to see the 532 Blue Peter, write to the Blue Peter Locomotive Society, 116 Holgate Road, York. By the way, the Blue Peter Locomotive Society has no connection with our programme, but Peter was very honoured indeed when he was asked to become Vice President.

At the end of 1970, a painting was put up for sale in London. For many years it had been in a private house, not an art gallery, so few people had seen it before.

It was called "The Moorish Slave" and it had been painted more than 300 years ago by the great Spanish painter, Velazquez.

At the auction, the picture was finally sold for £2,310,000. It was fantastic! A world record! No picture had ever been publicly sold for such a price before.

People were amazed at the price–but they were also puzzled by the picture itself.

"Who was he?" they asked. "This handsome, coloured man? How did Velazquez know him? Why did he paint his portrait?"

Then they discovered that the model had been a real person called Juan de Pareja. Something was known of his life, and many stories had been told about him.

Young Juan was half African, and he was a slave. He worked in the household of a family called Velazquez in Seville, Spain. Juan did the cleaning and scrubbing, and generally looked after the house. He expected to spend his whole life working in this way, but one day he was sent to Madrid to work for the son of the house–Diego Velazquez.

Velazquez was a painter who was becoming quite well known, and he needed an assistant. So now Juan learned to grind up the hard lumps of earth, used for colouring, to a fine powder. Then he mixed them with oils to make the paints Velazquez would use.

He learned to stretch canvas on wooden frames ready for a picture to be painted on it.

Each morning he made the artist's palette ready for him, with every colour in its right place, and every evening he washed out the brushes ready for the next day. All this was part of the work of a busy studio and Juan enjoyed it, but secretly he longed to paint for himself. Sometimes he stood in front of an empty canvas–brush in hand. But by the laws of Spain, no slave was permitted to paint pictures, or carve statues. No one was allowed to teach him to paint, and Juan was too scared to try by himself.

But Velazquez was a kind master and took Juan everywhere–even to the Royal Palace when he was asked to paint the King of Spain. King Philip was a sad, melancholy man, but he was interested in painting, and he became a real friend of Velazquez. When he was in the studio in the Palace, the rigid formal etiquette of the Spanish court fell away from him, and he would sit and

the Painter's Assistant

talk while Velazquez painted. And all the time Juan watched his master at work and tried to learn.

At last when the studio was empty, he would pick up ends of charcoal and scraps of paper, and try to draw and sketch as Velazquez seemed to do so effortlessly. Even if it was against the law, he felt compelled to go on.

One day the King commanded Velazquez to go to Italy with a Royal Embassy. There, he was to buy pictures for the King's palaces, and he would be able to see for himself the works of the great Italian artists. It was arranged that Juan would go too, for Velazquez would need a servant.

But when they had reached Rome, Velazquez became ill. He had a poisoned hand, and for several weeks he could not work, even though Juan looked after him carefully.

When he was getting better, a messenger arrived with a commission from the Pope himself, for Velazquez to paint his portrait. It was a great honour, but the artist was worried. He was afraid his hand might have lost its skill while he had been ill.

Suddenly he had an idea. "First, I shall paint you, Juan," he said. "It will help get my hand back into practice again, and I shall show your picture to everyone because you have been so good to me for all these years!"

So now Juan became a model, and Velazquez began his work. It was to be one of the best portraits he ever painted.

When it was finished, nobles and all the important men of Rome came to see it. They looked at Juan standing near to the portrait and they were amazed at the likeness, and the skill of the painting–so much so that many of the nobles ordered their portraits to be painted, too. Soon Velazquez painted the Pope, as he had been commissioned, and this, too, was considered a masterpiece. So altogether, the visit to Italy was a tremendous success.

But Velazquez and Juan were glad when they returned to their studio in Madrid, especially when the King came to look at the new canvasses they had brought back with them.

Suddenly the King stopped at one picture.

"What is this?" he asked.

Juan spoke up. "It is mine, Your Majesty," he said. "I have been painting secretly for many years, although it is against the law for a slave. I beg you to forgive me."

Troubled and perplexed, the King turned to Velazquez.

"What should we do with your disobedient slave?" he asked.

"Sire," said the painter, "before I answer, let me first write an important letter."

Quickly he wrote a few lines, and then immediately he put the paper into Juan's hand. It declared that Diego de Silva y Velazquez had freed his slave, Juan de Parejo, and appointed him as his assistant.

So now, as Juan was not a slave, he had not broken the law by painting! Juan, the King, and the painter himself were delighted at this way out of the difficulty.

Velazquez was now painting better than ever before, and he began work on his greatest picture. It showed the King's little daughter surrounded by her attendants, actually being painted by Velazquez, who himself appeared in the picture–the only self-portrait he ever painted. In a mirror the King and Queen could be seen watching the proceedings.

The King was delighted and thrilled by this exciting picture. One day, when it was nearly finished, he picked up Velazquez's paintbrush and painted a red cross on the doublet of the artist in the picture.

"Look," he said. "I have made you a Knight of the Order of Santiago, to honour you and your painting, and that cross is the badge of the Order."

And no one was more pleased than Juan, who was there in the background, just as he had been all through Velazquez's working life as chief painter to the Royal Court of Spain.

Now Velazquez is considered to be one of the greatest painters that ever lived. The wonderful painting of the princess with the artist is still in Madrid in Spain, and many countries and private collectors are proud to own some of Velazquez's other paintings. But not one has been auctioned for such a colossal amount of money as the portrait of Juan de Pareja, the painter's assistant!

Witches & Wizards

Can you turn someone into a toad? Can you cast spells? I'd be very surprised if you could! But here's a bit of magic anyone can work. Make a few magic passes over a dish-mop and a plastic lemon and you can transform them into a witch or a wizard. If you'd like to make special weird glove puppets, here's what to do:

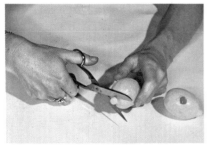

1 To make a witch's head, first cut the screw top off a plastic lemon. The pointed end will be the nose. Next, cut two holes, one at each side, just big enough to take the handle of a dish-mop.

2 Push the dish-mop handle right through the holes in the lemon and arrange the strands like straggly hair. If the mop hair is too thick, give your witch a haircut.

3 An easy way to make the face is to cut the eyes and mouth from black sticky-backed plastic. If you make the corners of the mouth turn down, your witch will look nice and nasty! If you want to paint the features instead, it's easiest to use enamel paint as this will stay on the plastic lemon best.

4 Fold an oblong of material in half and draw a witch's dress on it. Felt is a good choice as it won't fray when you cut it out. Make a tiny hole at the neck to push the dish-mop through. The dress should be long enough to hide the dish-mop handle and big enough for you to wear as a glove with one finger in one sleeve, and your thumb in the other. Sew or stick the side seams together and turn the dress the right side out.

5 To make the witch's hands, cut four mitten shapes from a different-coloured material. Sew or stick them together in pairs, but before you close the wrists, push a little stuffing inside to fatten them up. Then sew or stick the hands firmly into the witch's sleeves.

6 The stiff black paper hat is made in two pieces. First cut a fan shape, fold it into a cone, and glue down the edge. Next cut a circle for the brim. A cottage cheese carton lid makes a good pattern. Then cut a smaller circle inside, snip round the inside edge and bend up into little tabs. Glue the tabs inside the cone and decorate the finished hat with silver paper stars.

7 For a finishing touch, I've made my witch a cloak from an oblong of material. Put a hem down one long side, thread a piece of tape through, gather up the material and tie it round the witch's neck. You can glue on silver stars and moons to make it look witch-like. I've made her a broomstick, too, from a little bunch of twigs tied to a stick.

8 You can make a wizard in just the same way. When I trimmed his dish-mop hair, I saved the pieces to glue under his nose for a moustache and beard. Wizards' hats don't have brims, so I've glued the cone-shape straight on his head.
Use one hand to make your witch's arms wave and use the other to hold the dish-mop handle which makes her head nod. With a little practice you can make her cast spells!

Bleep and Booster

Bleep made a perfect landing, and in no time at all the boys were tucking in to the special birthday lunch that they'd brought with them. There were stellar paste sandwiches, lunar lollies and gravity cake, and a bottle of Asteroidade to wash it all down.

Booster swallowed the last crumbs and took his first good look round.

"This is a funny sort of place, Bleep," he said. "Where do you think we are?"

They had landed in a shallow, saucer-shaped crater at the mouth of what appeared to be a dried-up river. There were rocks and boulders everywhere, and a few strange bushes grew amongst them.

"No idea," replied Bleep. "But I know the bearings. I'll look it up in the Miron Commando Manual." And he ran back to the space pod.

Left on his own, Booster became uneasy. There was nothing to be seen; there was nothing moving on the edge of the crater, and yet he felt a hundred eyes were watching him. He began to feel quite scared and was relieved to see Bleep waving back to him across the crater, the Manual in his hand. But one look at Bleep's face told him that he wasn't the only one that was frightened.

"Oh, Booster," cried Bleep. "We're in great danger. Look!"

Booster grabbed the book. Horrified, he read "Bearing 075 green, 993 red. The planet Oozerus. Oozerus is inhabited by hostile monsters known as Oozeroids. Oozeroids attack on sight. This planet safe only during hours of darkness when monsters lose energy and are incapable of movement."

"It won't be dark for hours," cried Booster. "Let's get out of here!"

Together they tore across the crater, flung themselves, gasping, into the space pod and

Bleep's birthday had been a rotten one. He'd spent it in bed with a bad attack of the Greasles. His face had been covered with green spots and he'd felt really awful. The only thing that had cheered him up was his best birthday present, a pocket Suparay. It was only as big as a matchbox, but it was as power-packed as the ones issued to the Miron Space Commandos. At the flick of a finger, it could shoot a beam of bright, white light that could be seen from miles away—and what's more, the Suparay was everlasting and indestructible. No wonder Bleep was pleased with it!

The Suparay was in his pocket at this moment as, with Booster by his side, he skilfully manoeuvred the space pod between a cluster of asteroids and took his bearings on a nearby planet.

"What about landing there for lunch, Booster?" he asked. "We've never been there before."

"Right," said Booster. "Let's go!"

Both the boys were enjoying the flight, for it was a special one. This trip was Bleep's birthday treat. To make up for missing his party, the Captain had allowed Bleep to take the space pod out on a day-long flight, exploring anywhere they liked.

slammed the airlock door. Bleep flung down the rocket ignition switches and they braced themselves for take-off.

Nothing happened. There wasn't a flicker of response from any dial. An unseen force had crippled the space pod. Bleep and Booster were prisoners on a hostile planet!

Then, as they gazed helpless through the observation windows, a dreadful sight met their eyes.

Rolling slowly down the crater, and advancing threateningly towards them, were dozens of great glass spheres, and inside each one a huge and terrifying Oozeroid monster.

"Quick," cried Bleep, "the ray guns." They flung open the airlock and blasted away, but even though

they switched to double destructor power, nothing stopped the slowly rolling spheres.

"Oh, Booster, the rays cannot penetrate the spheres," cried Bleep. "The monsters will get us and there's nothing we can do."

"Oh yes there is," shouted Booster. "We'll make our own weapon. I know something that will smash them to bits! Get some rocks—as many as you can!"

"What for?" cried Bleep.

"No time to explain—just do as I say!"

While Bleep leapt from the space pod and grabbed at the boulders lying in the crater, Booster quickly tore off the elastic webbing straps that held his backpack. Then, as Bleep watched, amazed, he fixed each end to the side of the open air-lock door, loaded up with a rock, aimed and fired.

CRASH! Booster's giant catapult shattered a sphere at every shot.

"Oh, Booster!" cried Bleep. "What a brilliant new invention. In the whole of space there's nothing like it!"

"There may be nothing like it on Miron City, but it's just about the oldest weapon on Earth," explained Booster. "Quick, get some more ammunition. Here comes another lot!"

But Bleep's congratulations came too soon. Booster's catapult soon stopped the rolling spheres but now from every shattered wreck crawled an Oozeroid monster, its pincer-like claws rattling menacingly. Once more the boys grabbed the ray guns and fired desperately at the leathery bodies. For a moment, the Oozeroids hesitated, but finding themselves unharmed, they slithered and scrabbled inch by inch, closer and closer to the terrified boys.

"We need more power," cried Bleep. "If only our ray guns were stronger."

Booster thought desperately. "I think I've got it," he shouted. "Quick, get your Suparay and follow me!"

Unquestioningly, Bleep dashed after Booster as he hared across the crater, only inches from the monsters, and picked up the biggest chunk of broken sphere he could find. He turned it towards

the leading Oozeroid.

"Now, Bleep," he yelled. "Switch on the Suparay and aim through the glass."

Instantly, Bleep flicked the switch. The pencil-thin beam of light shone through the glass, magnified a thousand times, and caught the leading monster in a searing, white-hot beam. There was a sickening sizzle and the creature lay dead.

"Good work," exclaimed Booster. "Fire again!"

Over and over again, Booster aimed the lens and Bleep fired. Oozeroids writhed and twisted in the deadly beam until the crater was littered with corpses. Then, as suddenly as they'd come, the survivors retired, until Bleep and Booster could see nothing of them but row upon row of glaring eyes staring down at them from the crater's edge.

Exhausted, Bleep and Booster sank down behind a rock and held a hasty council of war.

"Look, Bleep," gasped Booster. "We've only one

shattered. A dreadful sight met their eyes.

While they'd been planning, they hadn't noticed that the Oozeroids had reformed. Now, on the edge of the crater stood the most enormous disintegrator gun they'd ever seen—and it was aimed directly at the space pod!

There was a high-pitched whine, a deafening explosion, and the space pod split from top to bottom, while from the two useless halves spilled a mass of mangled machinery. Only one thing seemed unharmed—the space scooter.

Recovering from the shock of the explosion, the boys scrambled towards it, but even as their eager hands reached out to grab it, a new terror struck. Pouring down the crater sides came thousands and thousands of gallons of water. The Oozeroids had struck again—this time with Hydro Cannons. The crater was filling up fast and their precious space scooter was washed against a rock and smashed before their eyes.

"Help, Booster! I'm drowning," cried Bleep. "Save me!"

Booster grabbed at his friend's antennae with one hand, and with the other clutched for support at a piece of bobbing wreckage. It was the top half of the space pod, now floating uselessly on the surface.

chance to escape. The space pod's useless, but the space scooter's inside and it's probably O.K. There might be enough fuel to get us to a nearby planet and from there we could radio for help. And if we shelter in the space pod until it's dark, the Oozeroids will be immobile and won't try to stop us!"

Both boys knew the plan was pretty hopeless, but they hid their fears from each other, determined to keep their spirits up. But as they crept out from behind their rock, all their hopes of escape were

"The space pod's gone, the space scooter's gone, the ray guns have gone, we're too far from home for radio contact. Oh, Booster, what shall we do?" sobbed Bleep.

"I'll think of something," said Booster bravely. "I always do."

He hadn't an idea in his head, but he knew that Bleep was counting on him, so he did his best to sound confident. Bleep cheered up at once. "At least, I've still got my Suparay," he said, and took the little box from his pocket. Booster sprang to his feet.

"That's it!" he cried. "You've got the answer. The Suparay can save us. Well done, Bleep!"

Bleep was mystified, but he helped Booster drag the space pod boat ashore as he was asked, and between them they propped it up on two big rocks. It stood there like a huge, shining dish.

"There you are," exclaimed Booster, delightedly. "The Bleep Patent Searchlight Reflector. Shine your Suparay on it, and there'll be a beam of light from here to Miron City. They're bound to spot your signal!"

Booster was right. The light from the Suparay Searchlight was dazzling, and in no time at all, they could see Space Freighter 9 right overhead, hovering in the guiding beam. Before light began to dawn, Bleep and Booster were safely on board.

"Well," laughed Booster, "I'll never forget your birthday treat—not as long as I live!"

"Nor shall I," agreed Bleep. "I think I'd rather have the Greasles! And there's something else I'll never forget—my Suparay! It may have been my worst birthday, but it's my best birthday present ever!"

"But it's not useless," thought Booster. "It can save us!"

With a tremendous effort he heaved Bleep's almost lifeless body into the shell, and breaking off a piece of the shattered instrument panel to use as a paddle, rowed as hard as he could away from the leering Oozeroids, down the gorge that led from the crater. Once on board, Bleep recovered. For hour after hour the boys took turns to paddle, until they were exhausted.

"We daren't stop, Bleep," said Booster. "Not until it's dark. I can hear the Oozeroids following us. We've got to keep going."

The awful noise of the monsters' scaly bodies scrabbling over the rocks echoed down the gorge behind them. But the gorge got narrower and narrower, and the water got less and less. Their plight was dreadful, for high above them, peering down the sides of the gorge, there were now hordes and hordes of Oozeroids.

Just as their frail craft scraped the bottom and they knew they could go no further, darkness came.

Bleep and Booster held their breath.

"Can you hear anything?" whispered Booster.

"No," Bleep whispered back. "They are immobile, just as the Manual said."

They huddled together in the darkness, desperate and afraid, and took stock of their dreadful plight.

The Friendly Dolphins

Would *you* feel like having a swim with a load of 600 lb. monsters, each with a mouthful of 90 gleaming white teeth? I had my doubts! But after spending only a few minutes with Belle, Prinny and Moby, I knew I was in the company of some of the friendliest and most fun-loving creatures in the world.

They're three members of a Dolphinarium—and with one of them called Prinny, it's easy to guess they're based at Brighton, home of the Prince Regent in the 18th century. The Prince was nicknamed "Prinny" by his friends—he didn't weigh 600 lb. although he *was* enormously fat, and he, too, was friendly and fun-loving.

Some people don't approve of circuses because they think wild animals should be left in their natural surroundings and not taught to do tricks. But dolphins are different. Anyone who's been on a boat and watched a school of dolphins trying to race them, and performing incredible acrobatics at the same time, will tell you that they're great show-offs. They love doing tricks and pleasing human beings.

"The worst thing you can do to a dolphin is to ignore him," said one of the trainers at Brighton. If a dolphin behaves badly at the Dolphinarium, all the trainer has to do is to turn his back for a few moments, and the dolphin will immediately start to co-operate.

So when you visit Prinny and his friends, you see an actual show—a selection of the dolphins' favourite tricks, and I was lucky enough to be asked to join their trainer in the water for one of their performances.

The whistle I'm blowing is the signal for Belle, Prinny and Moby—to collect their rewards—chunks of smelly mackerel!

I used a big bath brush to clean Prinny's teeth. It had to be a big one—a fully grown dolphin has between 80 and 90 teeth.

Before the show began, I was introduced to the "stars"—and I *mean* introduced. As soon as I held out my hand, Prinny shot across the pool like an arrow and shook flippers!

I swam around with them for a bit and we all got used to each other. The seats had filled up by now, so the show was introduced and the dolphins' signature tune blared out over the loud speakers. It was Puppet on a String—and the dolphins are so intelligent, they've learnt to recognise the music. Like lightning they began their act, which started with jumping. It's quite impressive watching 600 lb. of mammal leaping 16 feet in the air—and they do it extraordinarily gracefully.

After each jump, the trainer blew his whistle, which was the signal for the dolphins to collect their rewards—large chunks of smelly mackerel. These rewards are very important, and none of the dolphins is ever missed out.

Dolphins have to come out of the water to breathe. They're mammals, of course, not fish and they breathe through a round opening in the top of their head called a blowhole. It's like the breathing hole a whale has, and when they submerge, a special flap immediately covers it up and keeps it watertight. They can stay under water for as long as 7 minutes, but usually they surface every 30 seconds or so.

The rubber rings trick came next. There were several rings, all different colours. The dolphins had them on the ends of their long noses and we had to try and grab them back. When I made a dive for Moby, I got hold of the ring all right, but she was so strong, she just towed me around the pool—pulling me like a piece of driftwood.

There was another big laugh from the audience when I cleaned Prinny's teeth! I used a big bath brush with a long handle—and it was a good thing the brush was a large one. Although baby dolphins are born toothless (like human babies), fully grown ones have between 80 and 90 spiked white teeth! But the reason they always look so cheerful isn't because they're smiling, but became of the natural curve of their mouths. When I'd finished cleaning their teeth with special mackerel-flavoured tooth paste, I held up a big board with the word RINSE on it. To everyone's astonishment, that was exactly what the dolphins did—splashing the water around with a great deal of noise.

There were dozens more tricks—including a football match which I would have enjoyed more if I hadn't had to keep goal *and* feed the dolphins at the same time. And Prinny's famous balancing act. He glides upright on his tail at colossal speed right down the whole length of the pool—and while the audience is rubbing its eyes in amazement, he circles back and does a lap of honour—all at about 35 m.p.h!

But the grand finale starred Belle. I climbed a ladder that was suspended right out over the pool. When I was about 16 feet up in the air, I held out an extremely small hoop—only fractionally bigger than the width of Belle's body. It would have needed only the slightest miscalculation for the trick to have failed—but with a stupendous leap, Belle soared into the air and through the hoop without even brushing her skin against the edges. And with the cheers of the crowd ringing round the pool, she thoroughly deserved the large whole mackerel she was given as a reward.

The reason why Belle was able to judge her leap so exactly, and why none of the dolphins ever collide in the pool—even though they move so swiftly—is because they have their own built-in homing devices. As a matter of fact—their sonar system is ten times more accurate than radar. A dolphin can transmit a series of impulses at any object in its path—say a ball or a piece of mackerel, or the side of a ship. When the impluses hit the object and signals are returned, the dolphin can compute them into size, shape and distance.

Dolphins also have their own language. It's a series of very complex whistles and squeaks, and experiments have shown that when two dolphins are talking, they wait for each other to finish before interrupting. Scientists have identified an S.O.S. whistle, but so far, that's about all they've been able to translate. They've even discovered that by the time he was two months old one baby dolphin was taught over 600 different "words"! It's just possible that one day men and dolphins will be able to communicate using this language—something that has never yet been known to happen in the whole history of man.

Next time I'm asked to join the dolphins in their pool, I certainly won't have any fears. They're easily the most fascinating creatures I've ever met—and in spite of the fact they're strong enough to be shark killers, Prinny, Moby and Belle were just as gentle and friendly as Petra and Patch.

Pete says "Why didn't I keep my big mouth shut"

When I first joined Blue Peter, they asked me what outdoor things I liked best.

"Football," I said, "but I don't play it very well."

"Well—what are you good at?" they persisted.

"I don't know—I'm not bad at swimming," I said modestly.

Looking back on it now, I think those were about the stupidest words I ever uttered.

Not that I minded swimming in the tropical waters of Mexico and Ceylon, and I raised absolutely no objection to the heated diving pit at the National Sports Centre at Crystal Palace.

But the English Channel in November wasn't what I had in mind when I said I was keen on swimming.

It all started when we read in the papers one day that the Woodberry Down Boys' Club—average age 14 years—had successfully swum the Channel in 14 hours 10 minutes. Instead of one person ploughing across the 21 miles between Dover and Cap Gris Nez, six of them had swum it in relay. According to the Swimming Association rules, each swimmer has to be in the water for exactly an hour at a time, and they must swim in strict rotation.

One cold, grey morning last November, Val, John and I joined the Woodberry Down Boys' Club on the beach at Dover. No one in their right mind would attempt to

According to the rules, the water temperature must be taken—it was 52 degrees Fahrenheit!

swim the Channel in November, which might explain why we were doing it. We never seriously thought we'd go the whole way, but we just wanted to find out for ourselves what Channel swimming was all about.

It started off by the first contestant (P. Purves) being smeared from head to foot by his team-mate (J. Noakes) with some evil-smelling white grease, which was supposed to keep the cold out.

To find out exactly how much cold we were going to contend with, Mike Morford, the Channel Swimming Association Observer, was testing the temperature of the water—it was 52 degrees Fahrenheit, two degrees warmer than the air temperature.

After Johnny, snug in his warm track-suit, had finished plastering me with hard, stinking grease, I waded out alone into the icy waters of the English Channel. No wonder they call swimming the loneliest sport in the world!

There are those who claim that once you're over the first shock, your body gets used to the cold and you can stay in for ever—the "Come on, it's all right when you're in" brigade. Well, I've got news for them! After ten minutes I just couldn't stand it for another stroke, so I shouted for the next swimmer to take over. The rules state that the relief swimmer must be in the water before his mate is allowed to touch the boat, and he must dive in *behind* him, so that every yard of the Channel is actually swum.

I don't think I've ever been so cold in all my life. Val was waiting for me on the boat with hot tea, hot towels, and a dressing-gown. I knew the Blue Peter cameras were turning over, and that everybody was waiting for me to give a brilliant description of the swim. I opened my mouth—but nothing came! I just couldn't speak for sheer, agonising cold.

Johnny, snug in a warm track-suit, started to cover me with evil-smelling grease.

No wonder they call Channel swimming the loneliest sport in the world!

Whilst I was in the water, Johnny thought he'd let someone else "volunteer" to be next in the relay.

After ten minutes I'd had enough— I just couldn't stand it for another stroke.

I don't think I've ever been so cold in all my life. I was literally shaking from head to foot.

Eventually, Val's hot tea did the trick, and I began to feel human again. As the feeling came back to my limbs, the first thought to enter my mind was "If I've done it, I'm going to make sure that star of tropical waters, John Noakes, has a go as well!" So I put on an anorak and went on deck to look for him.

It didn't take very long. There, sitting in the bow, with a wan smile, and his face a delicate shade of lime green, was Johnny.

"When are you going in?" I said, heartlessly.

He turned to me and smiled again, but a bit more desperately than before. His face looked like an out-of-focus picture.

"I'm feeling a bit poorly, Pete," he said, then swung round and stuck his head over the side again.

By this time everybody was frozen, and almost everybody was sick, including the Blue Peter camera team.

The only person who wasn't feeling ill was Val, who, for reasons that no one could understand, remained cheerful and looked marvellous throughout. She couldn't understand why no one wanted her bacon sandwiches!

"Are you going back already?" she said to the wretched, frozen crew. "I was just beginning to enjoy myself!"

Val's hot tea began to revive me— and as the feeling returned to my limbs, I had one thought in my mind. "If I've done it, Noakie's going to have a go!"

I found him sitting in the fo'c'sle with a wan smile on his face, which was a delicate shade of green. "When are you going in?" I asked brutally.

"I'm feeling a bit poorly, Pete," and then he swung round and stuck his head over the side. I didn't have the heart to ask him again.

The Lion and the Mouse

I met plenty of lions on my Blue Peter Royal Safari—from the safety of our Safari Land-Rover. We've had several cubs in the Blue Peter studio, and I've taken quite a large lion for a walk. But a few months ago, I met my most remarkable lion of all: an Asian lion called Leo, whose best friend is five thousand times smaller than himself—a tame white mouse! Come to think of it—perhaps it's the *mouse* who's remarkable. After all, one slight flick of Leo's gigantic front paws and she'd be completely crushed.

Quite honestly, unless I'd seen them with my own eyes, I don't think I'd have believed it. But Blue Peter cameras were there to record what happened—so there's positive proof that this isn't just a tall story.

Leo was 18 months old when I met him. He belongs to Mr Roy Clarke of Wellingborough, who says that he's completely and utterly tame. This may be because when he was only two days old his mother deserted him, so he was hand-reared, and at first he had to be bottle-fed every two hours with glucose and milk. Now, 18 months later, Leo weighs over 300 lb., eats 11 lb. of beef each day, and has 8 daily pints of milk.

His teeth look enormous—but Mr Clarke says he's never bitten anyone—and he is tremendously strong, so playing with him can turn into a pretty rough game—although Leo doesn't intend to do any harm.

Matilda's been Leo's friend for the last nine months. It all began when she gnawed her way out of her box and disappeared. After a search that went on for several hours, no one thought she'd ever be seen again. But suddenly, Mr Clarke spotted her by Leo's cage. Immediately he rushed to her rescue and reached out to try and grab her—just as Matilda scuttled through the bars. But to everyone's surprise, Leo *didn't* pounce. Instead, he let Matilda climb over his paws, up his enormous furry head, and into the long hairs of his mane. He actually seemed to enjoy it—showing not even the slightest signs of wanting to snap at her with his enormous teeth—and ever since then, Matilda and Leo have been firm friends.

Sometimes Leo and Matilda go for walks together—and whenever Matilda's tired, she just hitches a lift and rides the rest of the way in comfort on Leo's back. So if someone says to you "By the way, guess what I saw the other day? A white mouse sitting on a lion's mane!"—don't be *too* disbelieving—after all, it may have been Leo and Matilda out for a stroll.

Veteran Car Run

This is the magnificent 1903 Cadillac we drove in the 1970 London to Brighton Veteran Car Run.

7.55 a.m. Hyde Park, London. The crowd gave us a good send-off as we took up our position amongst the other 250 entrants at the starting line.

9.00 a.m. As Big Ben chimed, we were on schedule over Westminster Bridge and a passing car gave us a friendly wave.

1.00 p.m. We'd been driving now for over four hours but there was no time to stop if we were to reach Brighton by 4.00 p.m.

2.30 p.m. Every few yards of our 54-mile journey there were always Blue Peter viewers to cheer us on and encourage us.

3.59 p.m. The Sea Front, Brighton. With just one minute to spare, we made the finishing line to qualify for a special medal!

The CADILLAC of 1903

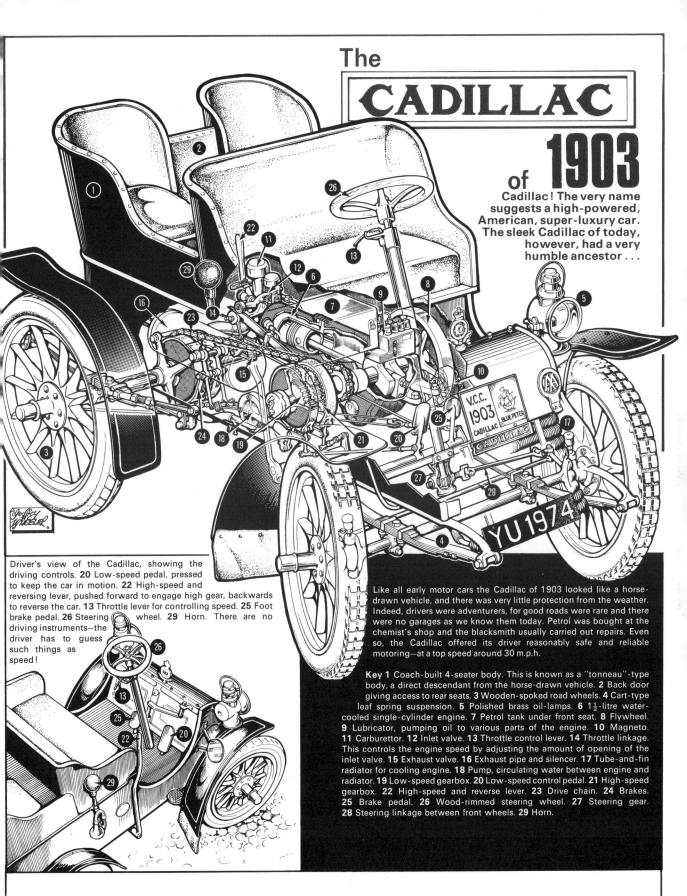

Cadillac! The very name suggests a high-powered, American, super-luxury car. The sleek Cadillac of today, however, had a very humble ancestor . . .

V.C.C. 1903 CADILLAC

BLUE PETER

CADILLAC

YU 1974

Driver's view of the Cadillac, showing the driving controls. **20** Low-speed pedal, pressed to keep the car in motion. **22** High-speed and reversing lever, pushed forward to engage high gear, backwards to reverse the car. **13** Throttle lever for controlling speed. **25** Foot brake pedal. **26** Steering wheel. **29** Horn. There are no driving instruments—the driver has to guess such things as speed!

Like all early motor cars the Cadillac of 1903 looked like a horse-drawn vehicle, and there was very little protection from the weather. Indeed, drivers were adventurers, for good roads were rare and there were no garages as we know them today. Petrol was bought at the chemist's shop and the blacksmith usually carried out repairs. Even so, the Cadillac offered its driver reasonably safe and reliable motoring—at a top speed around 30 m.p.h.

Key 1 Coach-built 4-seater body. This is known as a "tonneau"-type body, a direct descendant from the horse-drawn vehicle. **2** Back door giving access to rear seats. **3** Wooden-spoked road wheels. **4** Cart-type leaf spring suspension. **5** Polished brass oil-lamps. **6** 1½-litre water-cooled single-cylinder engine. **7** Petrol tank under front seat. **8** Flywheel. **9** Lubricator, pumping oil to various parts of the engine. **10** Magneto. **11** Carburettor. **12** Inlet valve. **13** Throttle control lever. **14** Throttle linkage. This controls the engine speed by adjusting the amount of opening of the inlet valve. **15** Exhaust valve. **16** Exhaust pipe and silencer. **17** Tube-and-fin radiator for cooling engine. **18** Pump, circulating water between engine and radiator. **19** Low-speed gearbox. **20** Low-speed control pedal. **21** High-speed gearbox. **22** High-speed and reverse lever. **23** Drive chain. **24** Brakes. **25** Brake pedal. **26** Wood-rimmed steering wheel. **27** Steering gear. **28** Steering linkage between front wheels. **29** Horn.

Every year, in early November, old cars like this Cadillac take part in the London to Brighton Veteran Car Run but what are they celebrating? Until 1896 the law insisted that a man carrying a red flag had to walk ahead of all cars (and other forms of mechanical road transport) to warn people of the danger of the oncoming vehicle. This meant that besides having to pay a man to carry the flag, the motorist could only travel at a walking pace. No wonder then, when the Red Flag Act was scrapped in 1896, motorists celebrated by organising an "Emancipation Run" and driving down to Brighton in style. And they've continued to do this every year since!

Picnic Pasties

Do you get bored with sandwiches at picnics?

Why not have a change and make a savoury pasty like the one I'm eating. It's very quick and easy, and you can put your favourite filling in the middle. I like mashed sardine and hard-boiled egg best, but tomato and sausage is delicious, too, and you can probably invent lots more. You can even make a sweet pasty by using a banana and apple mixture, but don't sprinkle this with grated cheese—use brown sugar instead.

You don't *have* to make the pasty for a picnic—served hot from the oven, it's a really delicious dish for tea-time or supper!

Ingredients
12 oz self-raising flour *(340 grammes)*
4 oz fat of any kind *(113 grammes)*
¼ oz salt *(7 grammes)*
Enough milk to make a soft dough.

Filling
This can be sardine, tomato, sausage, hard-boiled egg, chopped cooked bacon—pretty well anything you like!

1 Put the flour, fat and salt in a mixing-bowl and knead into a dough using a little milk (yogurt will do instead). It should be soft, and just thick enough to roll out.

2 Divide the dough into two pieces and roll each one out into two equal-sized oblongs about ½" thick. (Remember to flour your board and rolling-pin first to prevent the dough sticking.)

3 Pour a little melted fat on a baking-sheet and sprinkle with flour. Put one dough oblong on the sheet and cover with filling. I'm using cooked sausage and tomato here. Leave a small empty "margin" all the way round.

4 Put the second dough oblong on top and pinch the edges together where you've left the "margin". Brush the top with milk and sprinkle with grated cheese to stop it becoming too dry.

5 Using an oven cloth, put the pasty in an oven heated at Regulo 6 (gas) or 400 degrees (electricity). Cook for at least 20 minutes, and take great care not to burn yourself when you lift the hot baking-sheet out of the oven.

6 Serve hot or cold. You can leave the pasty uncut if it's easier to pack this way in your picnic basket, or else cut it into slices. John and Peter thought my picnic pasty tasted great!

Radio Dogs

I don't recommend anyone to lose their way on a remote mountain in North Wales. If you *do*—at best you'll struggle back to base tired, footsore and hungry, and hours late. At the very worst you might stumble in the mist and break an arm or a leg and be forced to spend an uncomfortable night in the freezing cold before you were found, half-dead, by a search party. Many people don't realise how extraordinarily treacherous mountain weather can be. One moment the sun is shining and there's a warm breeze, but within seconds rain clouds can appear and fog can suddenly blanket the surrounding countryside. But I was lucky—high on the rocky slopes near Snowdon my calls for help were answered by a unique service— Mrs McCarthy's Radio Dogs!

Matilda to the Rescue

If someone had told me that one day I'd be rescued half-way up a mountain by a dog called Matilda, I'd have said they were barmy. But this is what my rescuer was called, and Matilda is one of a team of Great Danes trained and owned by Mrs Ruth McCarthy. Round Matilda's neck she wears what looks like a complicated sort of collar—it's actually a two-way radio which enables Mrs McCarthy to keep in touch with her and the other dogs who have identical radios, wherever they roam when they're out on rescue missions. Sometimes the dogs come across exhausted climbers quite by chance. Sometimes call for help echo over the hills and are picked up by sharp-eared Mrs McCarthy in her tiny cottage. At once, it's Action Stations—a team member is sent out, no matter

A cry for help echoes over the mountains, and Mrs McCarthy alerts one of her team of Great Danes.

I couldn't believe my eyes! I'd just about given up hope when along panted Matilda.

This is the remarkable notice I read on Matilda's two-way radio collar.

Eagerly I spoke into the microphone while my rescuer waited patiently.

Four miles away my calls for help were picked up on Mrs McCarthy's radio receiver.

Matilda led me safely to Mrs McCarthy's cottage. This Rescue Service is unique in Britain.

whether it's day or night, foggy, snowing, or raining cats and dogs. With their tremendously sensitive ears and noses, it's not long before the dogs discover the lost person— and no doubt all the other climbers and hikers in distress are as surprised as I was, when 120 pounds of panting Great Dane comes bounding along out of the seemingly uninhabited landscape.

Even though I was so tired, the first thing I noticed was Matilda's collar—you couldn't really miss it. Next I read its extraordinary label: **"This dog is a friend, you can trust her. If lost, press button on microphone and speak."** I did just that.

"Hello, hello. I'm wet and cold and I'm lost."

To my utter amazement a voice said:

"Radio Ruth answering. Are you hurt?"

"No," I replied truthfully, for

although I was exhausted and aching in every limb, I hadn't actually broken my leg or my ankle.

"Good," was the answer from Radio Ruth. "Now, will you please tell me the number on the dog's collar."

It was number one.

"Thank you," came the voice over the microphone. "Underneath the dog's neck there is a ring. If you pull it, you will find a lead."

"Yes, I've found it." I replied.

"Will you put the dog on to me please," asked the voice.

"Yes," I said incredulously and shoved the microphone near one floppy ear.

"Thank you," said the voice, and then it raised its tone. "Matilda! Matilda!" it called, "Come home Matilda!"

Without a moment's hesitation, Matilda was off, with me hanging on to the other end of her lead. I wasn't

risking letting go for a moment! Matilda seemed to know all the short cuts, and soon we'd left the mountain behind and were striding over rough grass and scrub-land. We'd walked about four miles when a cottage came in sight—and there was "Radio Ruth," herself, waiting to meet me. Mrs McCarthy gave me the best cup of tea I've ever tasted and I was able to dry my soggy, wet boots and trousers before setting off to return to my base.

No wonder I'm sold on the whole idea of Radio Rescue Dogs. It's still in its experimental days, but already it's proving enormously successful. Combined with the existing Mountain Rescue Services, it could be a means of helping even more people in distress.

Climbers lost on the north Welsh mountains stand a far better chance of being rescued, thanks to Matilda and her friends, and Radio Ruth!

Bedtime for Jason

Jason likes luxury, and we make sure he gets it. Every night we put him to bed in a washing-up bowl. But it's no ordinary bowl. We've converted it into a super luxury softly padded bed. Here's how to make one just like it.

First of all, stand the washing-up bowl on a piece of foam plastic and draw all round it. Cut out the shape and you will find it fits into the bottom of the bowl. Then, lay an oblong of material inside the bowl and let the edges overlap enough to allow for a hem all round. There will be too much material at the corners, so cut away the extra pieces. Next, make a hem big enough to take a length of elastic, then lay the material down wrong side up and pin the foam plastic shape right in the centre. Sew it firmly into place and then run the length of elastic through the hem on the material and tie the ends in a knot. Now you will have a padded washable cotton cover that you can slip over the washing-up bowl to convert it into a pet's super bed. The elastic will hold it firmly in place under the rim.

Cats like Jason will love their new bed, and so will kittens, puppies, or even small dogs.

Mystery Picture

Colour the spaces as indicated by the numbers and the picture will appear

1 Light Brown
2 Dark Brown
3 Black
4 Yellow
5 Light Green
6 Red
7 Light Blue
8 Dark Green
9 Dark Blue

37

Two's company but Three's a crowd

It was an awe-inspiring moment! We held hands and stared into the glass. There were John, Val and Pete holding hands with John and Val and Pete, who were holding hands with John and Val and Pete—and what's more, we were surrounded by an endless crowd of Johns and Vals and Petes! We could hardly believe our eyes! We were the victims of a giant-sized optical illusion. It was all done by mirrors. To get this peculiar effect, the three of us stood in the middle of a triangle of huge mirrors. We held hands with our reflections and found we'd become the pattern in a kaleidoscope.

A kaleidoscope is good fun. With two handbag mirrors and some old picture cards you can make endless patterns. Here's a special pocket kaleidoscope that you can make for yourself.

1 To make a kaleidoscope you will need two handbag mirrors, a cork and a small cardboard packet for the base. One that has held custard powder or blancmange is just the right size. Cover the box with a piece of sticky-backed plastic, but leave one end open so that you can store the mirrors and pictures inside.

2 Get two handbag mirrors and stand them upright at right angles. Fasten them together with sticky tape "hinges"

3 Stand the mirrors upright at a right angle on top of the box and mark their position very carefully. It's well worth checking the right angle with a set-square as the more accurate it is, the better patterns you will get from your kaleidoscope.

4 To hold the mirrors in place, first cut two sections from a cork. Cut a littie slot in each just big enough to slide a mirror in. Stick a cork at each end of the right angle you have marked on the box.

5 Old Christmas cards, postcards or pictures cut from magazines and glued on to thin card, all make good kaleidoscope patterns. With a pair of compasses, draw a circle on the cardboard. The diameter should be roughly the same measurement as the width of the box.

6 Put a drawing-pin through the little hole in the card that the compasses have made and pin it on top of the box. Make sure the picture doesn't touch the corks, or you won't be able to turn it easily.

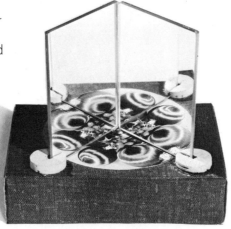

7 Slot the mirrors in position, and your kaleidoscope is all ready to use. If you save up your old Christmas and birthday cards, you can add more circles to your collection and every time you turn them you will get hundreds and hundreds of different patterns.

World Records

On Blue Peter, we've broken not just one, but *two* World Records!

First of all, on 18 May 1970, Holly Grey came to the studio and smashed the World Plate Spinning Record. He kept 43 china plates spinning simultaneously and didn't even chip one! This was tremendous, but our next record-breaking attempt was even more spectacular.

On 12 November 1970, I drove a small, 1200-c.c. Volkswagen into the studio. As I stepped out, students from the Bournemouth College of Technology started to pile in. First they lay on the floor, then they squashed into the boot. As more and more people crammed on top, you couldn't put a pin between the bodies. Just how many people *can* you get in a small saloon car? The world record stood at 64, but these students were determined to smash it. In seconds they were hanging out of the windows, stacked three deep on the roof and squashed against the steering-wheel. And yet to break the record, that car had to drive! Official Marshals, Ross and Norris McWhirter, Editors of the famous Guinness Book of Records, stood by to see that everything was done to World Record standards. As the students climbed in, I started to count. After a few minutes, I thought I must have made a mistake.

"How many on board?" I shouted.

"One hundred and two," was the staggering reply from the Marshals.

If I hadn't seen it with my own eyes, I'd never have believed it! Now came the big moment. I did a lightning calculation. That car must have been carrying a load of about five tons! How could it possibly move? Unless it could travel five metres, the record-breaking attempt wouldn't be recognised.

"Drive!" I shouted, and jumped on. Now there were ONE HUNDRED AND THREE on board!

There was a pause. The engine sprang to life, the car shuddered, and absolutely nothing happened. It was a sickening moment. Then suddenly the car inched forward. One metre . . . two . . . were they going to make it? I hardly dared look, then, all of a sudden, it shot forward, passed the five-metre mark, and juddered to a halt.

"We've made it!" I yelled.

In our Blue Peter studio yet another World Record had been absolutely shattered!

CLK 392B

Bengo

Three stories
without words
by Tim

Marie
Antoinette
Queen &
Shepherdess

When Louis XIV, the Sun King of France, built the Palace of Versailles, everyone who was anyone in the whole of Europe wanted to go there.

1 In Austria, hundreds of miles away, a 14-year-old princess called Maria Antonia was told that she was to marry the grandson of King Louis XIV of France. Maria Antonia had never seen him, but she knew that a princess must marry for the good of her country— not to please herself. One day, she would become the Queen of France.

2 The great bridal procession left Vienna. Her coach was piled high with flowers and followed by 57 coaches drawn by 340 horses.

3 After weeks of travelling, they reached the River Rhône—the frontier of France where a wooden pavilion had been built for the bride to meet her French court.

4 Inside the pavilion she changed into her French clothes and left behind everything that was Austrian, including her faithful servants. From now onwards she was French, and everything about her must be French. She had a new name—Marie Antoinette of France.

5 Several days later in a forest clearing, she met the shy young man who was to be her husband, and who one day would become the King of France.

6 They drove in the Royal coach together, and at last she saw the great golden gates, and the glittering magnificence of Versailles spread out to welcome her.

7 She never left the Palace again, for more than a few days at a time, for everyone and everything came to Versailles. Ceremony, amusement and dress were the most important things in her life.

8 Every morning, vast pattern books containing material samples of all her thousands of dresses were brought to her bedside so that she could choose what to wear that day.

9 She set a style of hair dressing with hair piled up high from her forehead and stiffened with heavy pomade.

10 All the ladies of the court followed suit—and soon the doorways in the Palace had to be made higher, and some ladies even had to kneel down in their coaches to prevent their hair from hitting the roof.

11 Because it was such a trouble to redo, the hair was sometimes left for days without recombing. It is even rumoured that mice, attracted by the heavy pomade, made their nests in the ladies' hair.

12 Marie Antoinette had everything in the world a girl could wish for. Her riches were beyond belief. But ceremony and rich dresses are not everything. They cannot fill up a whole life. Marie Antoinette was bored to death.

13 The only thing she had never tried was being an ordinary person—a peasant girl working on her father's farm—so she built her own little village a couple of miles away from the great Palace.

14 There was a little mill with flour ground by a water wheel in the stream—but the stream had been specially dug by a hundred labourers, and the water brought in pipes from miles away.

15 In the cowshed, she milked two pretty cows called Blanchette and Brunette. The cows were washed and groomed before she got there, and their milk fell not into wooden pails, but into buckets made of exquisite Sèvres porcelain, with the Queen's own initials on the side.

16 The lucky sheep, their wool washed to dazzling whiteness, were not driven to pasture, but guided on silk ribbons by the Queen of France herself.

17 Then, tired but happy, she rested in one of the cottages, except that inside it was furnished like a boudoir, looking more like a palace than a cottage. Yet Marie Antoinette believed that this was how the peasants lived.

18 But of course it was not. Real peasants were hungry, and worried and angry to hear of the Queen's extravagance. The Austrian Woman—they called her. The French people had never really accepted her.

19 At last the angry people of Paris stormed the gates of Versailles, took the King and Queen prisoner, and dragged them back to the city.

20 Marie Antoinette was executed in Paris, 15 miles from Versailles, by the people she had lived among for 20 years and never got to know.

A Car of the Future

Everybody who watches Blue Peter knows that I'm mad about cars. I actually built (with a little help from my friends) the car I drive every day to the Blue Peter studio.

That's why, when I heard that a revolutionary car of the future had been created by a famous French designer, I suggested that we took Blue Peter cameras to film it.

"It's a long way to go to look at a car," grunted the man at the BBC.

"Well, I could go up the Eiffel Tower, too," I replied hopefully.

Two days later I was standing in the middle of the famous Place de la Concorde, waiting for my first glimpse of the Automodule.

The designer, Jean Pierre Ponthieu, had told me on the phone that he would meet me on Sunday morning at ten o'clock. At least, that's what I thought he'd said, but as I don't speak French and he doesn't speak much English, by quarter past ten I was beginning to get a little apprehensive.

But I needn't have worried, because at twenty past ten there was a high-pitched chug-chugging, and from behind the Obelisk, one of the most ancient monuments in Europe, came the most fantastically modern thing I've ever seen on four wheels! I say on four wheels, but it was really on four legs with a wheel on the end of each instead of a foot. It looked, for all the world, as though something straight out of Bleep and Booster had shot from outer space and landed on the streets of Paris.

Jean Pierre Ponthieu leapt from the cockpit and shook my hand.

"Bonjour, John."

"Bonjour, Jean Pierre," I replied. So far my French was doing well, but I'd almost exhausted my vocabulary.

Jean Pierre beamed all over his face. "Eets a loffly day," he said with an air of triumph.

He looked as though he was from another world himself, but from the past rather than the future. He was wearing a beautiful purple velvet suit and a flowing white cravat. His hair was as long as Pete's, which is unusual in Paris because the average Frenchman goes in for short back and sides. But Jean Pierre wasn't an average anything, and soon we were both completely engrossed as he explained in a mixture of English and French, with a lot of gestures, why he had designed this extraordinary car.

"I wanted to design a car of the future–not like any other car that has ever been seen," he said. *"Par exemple*–what do you do when you have *difficulté* in parking? I show you."

He bounded back into the car and rapidly flicked half a dozen switches on a panel beside him. Immediately, the car began to rear up like a bucking bronco. "It *monte!*" he shouted triumphantly above the roaring engines.

The four legs closed together as the cockpit rose

higher and higher until the wheelbase was only taking up a fraction of the space it had occupied a moment before.

Jean Pierre slithered across into the passenger's seat, and gestured me to get in behind the wheel. I thought I could drive any sort of car in the world, but this one was all electrically controlled, so it was really like starting from the beginning again.

I was going to have to make a tricky manoeuvre to get past all the cars that had parked to see the Automodule.

"Does it have a good lock?" I asked hopefully. *"La tournée . . . ."*

"Ah, la tournée–un petit instant." He leant across and pressed a few more coloured switches.

"Voilà, the starteur." I pressed the button he indicated and the engine sprang into life.

"Vas-y! Vas-y! Please, please accelerate," he shouted.

I let the clutch out and pressed the throttle, and then, to my utter amazement, we moved off–not forward as I'd expected, but whizzing round and round in circles like a maddened blue-bottle. Jean Pierre fell about with laughter and then shouted.

"Arrête! Arrête!" I put my foot on what I hoped was the brake, and thankfully we stopped going round.

"Et maintenant," he announced, flicking a few more switches, *"l'autre tour. Allons-y!"*

I let the clutch out again and, sure enough, we belted round and round in the opposite direction. He'd certainly proved his point, the Automodule had a *very* good lock.

I looked through the window of the cockpit and there on the horizon I could see the Eiffel Tower, and I remembered my promise to the man at the BBC.

"Jean Pierre," I said. "Could you possibly give me a lift to the Eiffel Tower?"

"Avec plaisir," he said. "But I think better I drive."

"I think better you drive, too!" I said, and soon we were whirring along the beautiful Champs-Elysées, past the Place de l'Etoile, across the River Seine, to the foot of the most famous tower in the world.

1 Jean Pierre leapt out of the Automodule and in no time we were both completely engrossed as he told me all about his extraordinary car.

2 I climbed up beside him, and soon–to the amazement of other drivers–we were whirling round the Place de la Concorde.

3 As we drove up the Champs-Elysées we passed another peculiar car which Jean Pierre had designed.

The Symbol of the City

No matter where you go in Paris, you can't get away from the Eiffel Tower. It dominates the landscape and it has become the symbol of the City.

The man who built it, Monsieur Gustave Eiffel, used to dine every night in the first-floor restaurant. When asked why, he replied "Because it's the only place in Paris where you can't see the Eiffel Tower!"

The Eiffel Tower was originally built to be a symbol for a great exhibition to attract tourists from all over the world, and when the exhibition was over, they were going to pull it down.

Today the exhibition has gone, but the tower remains, and has become one of the greatest tourist attractions in the world.

When Gustave first presented his plans for a flimsy metal tower stretching 1,000 feet into the Parisian sky, the government of the day was absolutely horrified.

"But Monsieur Eiffel," one man said. "Are you sure it will work?"

Gustave looked at the plans again and said, "Probably not, but it will be fun to try."

Eventually he *was* allowed to try. The site was cleared and the foundations were dug. They went five metres deeper into the ground than the nearby River Seine.

Fifteen thousand separate pieces of metal were cast and brought to the site on great horse-drawn drays. They were bolted together by two and a half million rivets. It was like a giant Meccano set. The calculations were so exact that not a single piece of metal had to be altered, not a bolt enlarged.

Every morning, the 199 workmen climbed a bit higher to get to their work. They became so agile that they used to slide down their ladders like circus performers when it was time for them to go home in the evening. And in all the twenty months of building, there was not one serious accident to any workman.

As the sloping, threatening pylons reached higher, Parisians began to get alarmed.

A Russian officer rode a horse all the way from Warsaw—and right to the top of the tower!

"Will it stay up?" they asked.

By July 1888 the second platform was finished. The tower was beginning to take shape. But there were complaints.

"It's like a giraffe," said one critic.

"It's an inverted torch-holder," said another.

Meetings were held and petitions were launched demanding that "this hideous monstrosity—this dishonour to Paris" should be removed.

But the building went on.

Slowly, piece by piece, nut by nut, the great metal figure thrust upwards into the sky until at last it reached its full height.

On 15 May 1889 the Eiffel Tower was officially declared open by the Prince of Wales, who was later to be Edward VII of Great Britain.

Large crowds flocked to see the fantastic tower and a queue formed ready to go up; and today, eighty years later, the queue is still there. The clothes of the tourists have changed, but they still have the same ambition–to get to the top.

There's a lift that will take you all the way to the third stage, but I'd spotted the iron staircase running up the side and I remembered the Noakes family motto–"If it's there, climb it!"

When the tower was originally opened, the lifts weren't working. So the first visitors had to tread the same stairs I did–all one thousand seven hundred and ninety-two of them!

In fact, people used to vie with each other to find new and original ways to climb the tower.

A Russian Officer rode all the way from Warsaw on a horse, and then rode the horse all the way to the top. Another chap, a baker, climbed all the way up on stilts, and someone else rode all the way down on a bicycle.

When I reached the second stage, I'd had enough so I went up the last 525 feet by lift.

As we floated slowly up through the delicate steel structure, I felt the same excitement as millions of tourists had done before me.

At last I was there; I had reached the top. And, because 80 years ago Gustave Eiffel thought it would be "fun to try", I had, beyond doubt, the finest view of one of the most exciting cities in Europe.

monsters

Millions of years ago, in the days before there were any people, the world was ruled by the dinosaurs — the giant lizards that roamed the earth and lived in the swamps and strange primeval forests.

They were dead and gone long before men arrived, so they've never been seen alive by human eyes. And yet everybody knows exactly what they looked like, thanks to the detective work of naturalists and scientists. At museums you can often see actual skeletons of these amazing creatures, and it gives you a very funny feeling to stand underneath one. There's a Tyrannosaurus Rex at the Natural History Museum in London. When it was alive, it was the fiercest monster of them all, and if a man could have stood next to one, he would have just about reached to its knee. One day there's going to be a new monster on display there, and it'll be a special one for me because I'll have helped to put it there!

My monster is a plesiosaur. It's a giant sea creature, and guess where it was discovered? In Peterborough, which is nowhere near the sea! But 150 million years ago, there *was* sea where Peterborough now stands. Then the world changed and my monster was found on what used to be the ocean bed, with 40 feet of clay piled on top of it. It was discovered quite by chance when a workman was digging in the clay. There was a sudden "clink" and his shovel struck something solid. It turned out to be a giant bone. Soon a team of scientists from the Natural History Museum was on the site and after months of patient work, they revealed hundreds and hundreds of bones, which had lain hidden for 150 million years. Now, the scientists were planning to shift the whole skeleton back to London and they asked me if I would like to help. Of course I wanted to! A chance like this comes once in a life time, and I was off to Peterborough like a shot.

When I got down into the trench where the monster lay, I couldn't picture how they

1

2

Amazing discovery near Peterborough! 150-million-year-old sea
monster revealed!

1 These are the bones of a giant
plesiosaur and I helped to dig them
up–backbone, flippers and all!
2 Once this huge creature paddled
through the ocean, gnashing
its fierce teeth. Now it's going
to be a valuable museum exhibit.

Lots of monsters have been
discovered in Britain, weird
creatures like the pterodactyl
3 with its leathery wings and the
sharp-snouted fish-lizard *4*, the
ichthyosaur. In museums all over
the country you can see their
giant skeletons.

3

4

could possibly move this 15-foot giant. The plesiosaur seemed to have as many bones as a kipper – and if you can imagine taking a kipper to pieces, shifting it a hundred miles and then trying to put it together again, you'll have some idea of the problem!

But the scientists knew exactly how to tackle the job, and they didn't waste a moment. First of all the skeleton was photographed from every angle so that when the time came to put the bones together again, there would be a complete record of where every single piece went.

Then we started work, shifting the smaller bones. The plesiosaur got itself around by paddling along with giant flippers. Inside the flippers the bones were shaped like huge hands made up of lots of separate bones. Each one had to be scraped clean of clay, and I was told to be very careful over that job. The old bones were brittle, and if I'd been heavy-handed, I could have spoiled the whole skeleton. As I cleaned each bone, I had to wrap it in tissue paper, number it, and pack it in a crate, ready for the journey to London.

All the time I was working on the small bones, I was wondering how the scientists were going to deal with the big ones. I'd been told that the skull and all the dozens of bones that go to make up the backbone were to be moved in two great chunks, and I couldn't see how it was going to be done. But the team came up with a very ingenious answer. They built a cardboard wall up around the skull

and filled it with foaming polyurethane. In minutes it set hard, and there was the skull set in a solid plastic block, all ready for lifting. The same thing was done with the backbone, and soon we had a truck-load of bones all ready to be put together in London. It was a genuine Monster Construction Kit, and I'd helped to make it!

Although digging up and rebuilding monsters is a job for the experts, the first finds haven't only been made by scientists. The very first plesiosaur ever was discovered by an eleven-year-old girl. Her name was Mary Anning and her great discovery was made in 1811. She used to go looking for fossils on the beach at Lyme Regis, and she was just about the luckiest monster-hunter ever! She just seemed to fall over them, for not only did she discover the very first plesiosaur, but when she grew up she also discovered something else no one had ever seen before – a giant fish-lizard which was given the name ichthyosaur. And as if that wasn't enough, she went on to find the skeleton of a giant flying reptile, the pterodactyl – the first one ever found in the British Isles.

So you never know your luck! If you keep your eyes open, especially on the beach or in places inland where the sea *used* to be, you might just be as lucky as Mary Anning. You might find a monster too – because there may be hundreds of them lying around all over the world, just waiting to be discovered!

Mary Anning – Monster Hunter

"Having a marvellous time– wish you were here!"

This "postcard" doesn't exist–at least, the pictures are real enough–but you can't imagine anyone making them into a card, or anyone else wanting to send it to their friends.

Yet it's in filthy backstreets like these that hundreds of children have to play–not only at weekends, but during their school holidays, too. They never have the chance to go to the seaside or the country. Even their nearest park is miles away, and to reach their local swimming baths costs an expensive bus fare.

Quite honestly, if you're lucky enough to live in a house or flat that's in good repair, where you're close to fields or a park, and–even if you don't go away to the seaside, you sometimes stay with your Granny or your friends–it's hard to imagine what it must be like to live in a dilapidated street where perhaps half the houses have already been pulled down, and to have never ever had any kind of holiday in the whole of your life.

Strangely enough, what set the three of us thinking about this was our Giant "Blue Peter" Postcard Albums. Because of all the thousands of cards you've sent us, we now have seven giant volumes–and most of the cards are from "Blue Peter" viewers telling us of the terrific time they're having on holiday. There's certainly no doubt at all that people *enjoy* a holiday! It doesn't have to be an expensive one, or last a long time–it's the change as much as anything else that you appreciate–meeting new people and seeing new things.

It's easy to take having a holiday for granted, but we did some research, and were horrified to discover that in the really bad housing areas–which, unfortunately, are to be found all over Britain–there are hundreds of children who've never had a holiday in their lives.

"It's not fair," said John. "It's not their fault they live in a rotten dump with nowhere to play."

"I know people would want to help," said Val. "Anyone who's ever had a holiday would want to do something."

So we did some more research– this time to find out the best way in which we could help. It wasn't surprising to discover that holiday homes all over Britain had enormous waiting lists. But, even if they had enough money, most of the homes couldn't have extra rooms built on to them–either because there just wasn't the space, or because they couldn't get planning permission. It all seemed a bit hopeless– until we thought of Holiday Caravans. A big caravan–with room for 8 bunks could be parked in the garden of a Holiday Home. There'd be no need for special permissions, and the children could be looked after by staff who were already on the spot. Three of these mobile holiday homes could give over a thousand children a week's holiday each, every year.

"We'll need a lot of money," said Peter. "And I think I know how we can get it–spoons and forks!"

Peter was right. Spoons and forks melted down and turned into valuable metal ingots could be sold and the money used to buy our three caravans–but, and it was a big but, we'd need 200,000 parcels, each containing an average of half a dozen spoons and forks.

We thought–with *your* help, though–we might just about make it. As with all our "Blue Peter" Appeals, it's the small contributions that count. Not a few people sending colossal parcels, but masses of people sending small amounts of scrap commodities. Most people would be able to get hold of at least a few unwanted spoons and forks, and together, with a bit of luck, they might add up to the two hundred thousand we needed.

And how right we were! After announcing our great spoon and fork hunt on December 3rd, 1970, by our very next programme, 20,000 spoons and forks had reached our collecting depot. When we went down to help with the unwrapping, we were staggered—whole mountains of cutlery appeared with each special parcel delivery laid on by the Post Office. Nothing was wasted—brown paper, newspaper, string, stamps—they were all collected too, and another useful thing that went on at the depot was the magnet test. The most valuable metal we were likely to be sent was nickel silver. By holding a large magnet over the cutlery, we could separate this from the less valuable steel which, unlike the nickel silver, would cling to the magnets. Dividing it up meant nothing was wasted by being put into the wrong pile. (Some people very kindly sent us pieces of precious pure silver, and these were put aside too—not to be melted down, but to be sold separately at an auction.)

As the batches of spoons and forks were sorted, they were packed and loaded on to lorries and sent to a scrap metal factory in Curdworth, near Birmingham. At the factory, a second sorting took place—just in case any valuable spoons and forks had slipped through the net. Then, after laboratory tests, everything was shovelled into huge fiery furnaces—where the temperatures of over a thousand degrees centigrade soon dissolved the spoons and forks into molten metal. That was turned into ingots—some of which have probably been made into brand new spoons and forks by now!

Your response was fantastic! So much so that on December 31st, 1970, we were able to drive our three "Blue Peter" Holiday Caravans into the studio. And on January 4th we were able to make another important announcement! You'd sent us even more than our target of 200,000 spoons and forks, and with all the extra ones we were able to buy a "Blue Peter" Log Cabin. The idea was for the Cabin to be built in the grounds of a Holiday Home in Sunbury, where there happened to be plenty of space. There'd be 12 beds, and a special ramp for invalid chairs, so that disabled children who wouldn't be able to

1 At the Blue Peter Collecting Depot we helped to unwrap some of the hundreds and thousands of parcels of spoons and forks. Nothing was wasted—we even collected the brown paper, newspaper, string and stamps, too.

2 Our studio totaliser helped us to see how near we were to reaching our target.

3 At the scrap metal factory, a second sorting took place—to make sure we weren't melting down any valuable silver.

1 Your response was so fantastic
that we were able to drive our three
Holiday Caravans into the studio
on 31st December, 1970.

2 We delivered one of the Caravans
to Blackpool—one of Britain's
most famous holiday resorts.

manage the steps of a caravan
would still be able to have a
holiday. The exciting thing was,
that we were going to be able to
help to build the Log Cabin
ourselves–right from going to
Scotland and cutting down the
trees, to constructing the actual
Cabin. It's just like the houses
you find in Norway–the logs fit
together rather like a giant
construction kit. They're all
fire-proofed, and they keep you
cool in summer and warm in
winter.

It was very exciting to see our
Cabin grow–right from the
architects plans–and marvellous
to know that thanks to all your
parcels, even more children were
going to be able to have the first
holiday of their lives.

Once again we'd beaten all
previous records–by the end of
January our grand total of
parcels was over $2\frac{1}{4}$ million! Then
there was the result of our
Auction.

Altogether, the valuable silver
sent in by "Blue Peter" viewers
raised £796. But that wasn't all–

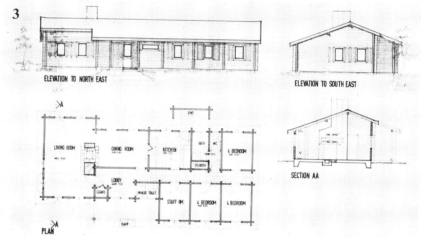

ELEVATION TO NORTH EAST

ELEVATION TO SOUTH EAST

SECTION AA

PLAN

3 These plans are the architect's
drawings of our Blue Peter Log
Cabin. The ramp is for invalid
chairs so that disabled children will
be able to have a holiday too.

the good news seemed to
snowball. One day the 'phone
rang in the "Blue Peter" office.

"It's the British Steel Corp-
oration here," said a voice.
"We'd like to give you two steel
houses–they're on show at the
Ideal Home Exhibition, if you'd
like to come and see them."

We were off like a shot! There,
at Olympia, we saw the two
houses. They were magnificent–
they didn't look as though they
were made of steel, they were
extraordinarily warm and cosy.
And after the Exhibition closed,
they, too, could be re-erected
very quickly like our Log Cabin,
and once put up on their
permanent site, they'd need far
less attention than houses made

from bricks and mortar.

It was all rather overwhelming
–counting the number of people
who'd be able to sleep in the steel
houses, we'd ended up being able
to provide holidays for nearly
3,000 children each year. For the
first time ever, these children will
be able to send holiday cards to
their friends, and thanks to *you*
they'll be able to write "Having a
marvellous time–wish you were
here!"

Life-boat News Flash

ROY COLE

BLUE PETER MEN STAND BY TO AID SURVIVORS

TWO Littlehampton lifeboatmen are on standby to go to the rescue of East Pakistan flood disaster victims.

They are Mr. Roy Cole, aged 45, of Clun Road, and Mr. Johnny Pelham, aged 43, of Pier Road. Both are crew members of Littlehampton's inshore rescue boat, Blue Peter.

The Royal National Life-boat Institution has sold 20 inshore boats to the Red Cross, who are sending them out to the Pakistan disaster area and crew members will be needed for them.

Already the institute's inspector of inshore boats and a mechanic are on their way to Pakistan and Mr. Pelham and Mr. Cole have been told to prepare to go out there in the next few days if they are needed. Both are quite happy with the arrangement.

Today they were both in London completing passport formalities. The Blue Peter rescue boat has been in Littlehampton for four years.

JOHNNY PELHAM

In November 1970, a terrible disaster struck East Pakistan–a 150 m.p.h. cyclone was followed by devastating floods. Five hundred thousand people were killed, and thousands more left homeless and starving. Emergency action was vital, and we were very proud when these two "Blue Peter" lifeboatmen were asked to help with the rescue operations.

Roy and Johnny flew out to the delta on 24 November and did invaluable work training the Aga Khan's scouts to handle the fleet of Inshore Rescue Boats provided by the R.N.L.I. and the Red Cross. These boats were identical to our Blue Peter craft, and were the only ones suitable for negotiating the shallow flood water, and transporting vital food and medical supplies to the victims of the disaster.

An eye witness report of the relief campaign was given to Blue Peter viewers when Roy and Johnny returned from East Pakistan and visited the Blue Peter Studio. They showed just how they had loaded the Inshore Rescue Boats for their life-saving mission.

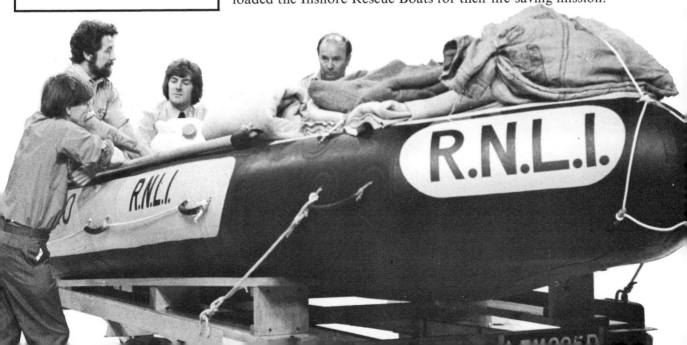

Paddington Weighs In

by Michael Bond
illustrated by "Hargreaves"

Paddington was most upset. Normally he was the sort of bear who took life very much in his stride, but for once things had taken a distinct downward plunge.

It all started when he arrived home late one afternoon only to find he'd missed almost the whole of a Blue Peter programme. Such a thing had never happened before, and what made matters even worse was the discovery that during his absence Val, John and Peter appeared to have been robbed of all their savings.

Paddington hurried into the lounge of number thirty-two Windsor Gardens and switched on the television just as the programme was drawing to a close. Rather frustratingly, the sound on the Browns' receiver always came on before the picture, so he only heard the news to begin with, but as far as he could make out Val had lost nearly a pound, Peter just over that amount, and John even more.

When the picture finally appeared on the screen it showed, rather surprisingly in the circumstances, a view of a new hotel which had recently been completed not far from Windsor Gardens and which the Blue Peter team had been visiting. But interesting though it was to see somewhere he actually knew, it was the following scene that nearly caused Paddington to fall backwards off his stool in astonishment, for it was only then that the full drama of the situation was revealed.

Val was lying on a mat in front of the camera, apparently recovering from shock, though fortunately still in a fit enough state to wave good-bye to the viewers at home. Peter, who obviously intended going for help, was shown in close-up sitting astride a bicycle–pedalling like mad, though for some odd reason he didn't appear to be moving. While John, who seemed to have come off worst of all, was suspended from a metal bar by means of a rope looped round one of his ankles.

Had it been any other programme Paddington might not have taken the affair quite so much to heart, but he'd got to know the Blue Peter team so well over the years–both by watching them on the screen and through visiting the studio on several occasions and meeting them personally–that it seemed almost as if he'd witnessed his own family being robbed.

Unfortunately, he was the only one to have seen the incident. Normally Jonathan and Judy, the Browns' two children, would have been there, but they were both away until the following evening. And with Mr Brown at his office, Mrs Brown busy sewing, and Mrs Bird–their housekeeper–even busier in the kitchen, there was just no one to talk to about the matter.

Even that night's paper didn't help. Paddington peered hopefully over Mr Brown's shoulder when he came across him reading it later that evening, but either the whole affair had happened too late to be included, or it had been hushed up, for there was no mention of it at all.

All in all, Paddington decided there was only one thing for it. He would have to visit the scene of the crime in person. He was a bear with a strong sense of right and wrong and he felt sure that even if he couldn't find the missing money he might well stumble across some kind of clue which might be of help.

As luck would have it an opportunity presented itself the very next day. With Christmas drawing near, Mrs Brown and Mrs Bird planned to do some shopping in the afternoon, and as a lot of it was secret and to do with Paddington himself it had been decided to leave him at home for once.

Only Mrs Bird felt uneasy about the matter. Paddington had displayed no interest at all in the cold lunch she'd set out for him, which was most unusual, and she had a nasty feeling he had something up his paw.

Had the Browns' housekeeper been able to see the note he propped up against the salad bowl soon after they left she would have felt even less happy.

It said simply: INVESTIGAYTING ROBBERY AT THE KNEW HOTELL. BACK LAYTER. PADINGTUN.

But by that time it would have been too late to do anything anyway, for Paddington was already heading down Windsor Gardens as fast as his legs would carry him.

There was a very determined expression on his face indeed. An expression that boded ill for anyone who tried to divert him from his chosen course, and one which was still present some time later when he crossed the foyer of the building he'd seen on Blue Peter and approached a man sitting behind the reception desk.

"I'd like to register, please," he announced importantly.

The man behind the desk looked slightly taken aback. "Er . . . we do executive week-ends," he said, running his finger down a large book in front of him while he played for time, "but we haven't exactly geared ourselves to taking in bears yet. I'm not sure if we have any vacancies."

"Oh, I don't want to stay a whole week-end," exclaimed Paddington hastily. "I have to get back to number thirty-two Windsor Gardens in time for dinner this evening. Mrs Bird won't like it if I'm late."

"Dinner!" For some reason the man raised his hands in horror at the very mention of the word, and he looked round hurriedly to make sure no one else had overheard. "Are you sure you've thought the matter over? We do like our guests to be in the right frame of mind."

"Oh yes," said Paddington earnestly. "I've been thinking it over all night. Ever since I saw what happened on Blue Peter."

"I know what went on," he added, lowering his voice, "and I've come to investigate the matter."

At the mention of Blue Peter the man seemed to have second thoughts about the situation. "Oh, well," he said, "in the circumstances I daresay we might arrange *something* for you."

He gave a slightly embarrassed cough as he looked Paddington up and down. "How many pounds did you have in mind?"

Crouching down in front of the desk so that the man couldn't see what was going on, Paddington opened his suitcase and felt inside the secret compartment.

"I think I could manage four," he said, peering into an envelope marked CHRISTMUS PRESENT MUNNEY. "Especially if I go without buns for a week or two."

The man rose to his feet, rubbing his hands in invisible soap. "I can see I misjudged you," he said enthusiastically. "You're obviously just the sort of client we like to have."

Crossing the hall he led the way down a long, white corridor lined on either side with doors.

Pausing outside one of them he removed a key from his pocket and placed it in the lock. "This is

your room," he announced, throwing open the door. "If you'd like to leave your things here I'll take you along to see our Mr Constantine. You might like to start off with one of his pummels."

Paddington licked his lips as he was helped off with his duffle coat. "Yes, please," he announced. "I think I'd like two if I may."

"Two of Mr Constantine's pummels!" The man gazed at Paddington with a look of awe. "Nobody's ever managed two at one go before. Are you absolutely sure?"

"Quite sure," said Paddington firmly.

"Well, I must say sooner you than me," remarked the receptionist in tones of growing respect. "Though I should warn you, if you feel like a bath later on you'd better come and see me first. I'll give you a plug.

"We can't be too careful," he added, seeing Paddington's look of surprise. "After only a very small pummel some of our visitors find they can't get out once they're in. We keep the plugs just to be on the safe side."

Paddington's eyes grew larger and larger. The walk to the hotel, combined with the fact that he'd gone without lunch, had made him feel even more hungry than usual. Mr Constantine's pummels sounded very good value indeed and his eyes glistened as he followed the man into the corridor and down a long flight of stairs.

Pushing open a pair of double doors the receptionist stood to one side to allow Paddington to pass through. "I'm afraid Mr Constantine doesn't speak a great deal of English," he remarked, pressing a buzzer to signal their arrival. "But I'm sure he'll be only too pleased to show you the ropes."

Paddington thanked the man for all his trouble. "I expect it's a bit difficult getting waiters these days," he said politely.

The ghost of a smile crossed the man's face as he made to leave. "You won't find any waiting with Mr Constantine," he chuckled. "He likes to get cracking straight away."

As the door closed behind him Paddington looked around the room with interest. He had been half expecting to find himself in a restaurant or at the very least some kind of canteen, whereas in fact, apart from a long, narrow couch in the centre, the room seemed completely bare of furniture.

Mr Constantine himself was also out of the usual run of waiters. He was the largest man Paddington had ever seen–almost as wide as he was tall–and apart from the fact that his dress consisted simply of a white singlet and trousers, much of his face was hidden beneath an enormous black beard.

Ignoring Paddington's greeting he emitted a series of grunts and then lifted him up onto a table, placing a hand like a bunch of bananas onto his head as he pushed him into a lying position.

Paddington hadn't had a meal in bed for a long

time and he lay back with a pleased expression on his face while he waited for the sheets to arrive.

Suddenly, to his alarm, Mr Constantine gave vent to a loud snort, rather like a wild elephant having a spot of bother with its trunk, and before he had time to call out for help, let alone make good his escape, he felt his legs being caught in a vice-like grip.

The receptionist had said that Mr Constantine liked to get cracking, but never in his wildest moments had Paddington expected his legs to be playing the leading role.

"Oooooooooo!" he yelled, as his assailant began working them up and down with all the enthusiasm of a parched explorer who has just stumbled on a water-pump in the middle of a sun-scorched desert. "Owwwwwwwwwwwwwww!"

"Urgggggggggh!" grunted Mr Constantine, beaming all over his face. "Is good, no?"

"No!" shrieked Paddington.

Mr Constantine nodded approvingly, another huge smile dawning as he landed on Paddington's stomach. "This is better, yes?"

"Yes!" yelled Paddington, growing more and more confused. "I mean . . . no! It's . . . huh . . . huh huh . . ." His voice died away in a long-drawn-out gasp, for either Mr Constantine was unable to take 'no' for an answer or his grasp of the English language fell a good deal short of the one he used on his victims.

It was all like a bad dream. The more Paddington shouted the more Mr Constantine seemed to take it as a signal that he was being called on for bigger and better efforts, though as Paddington's cries got louder and louder a look of concern gradually came over his face.

"You are not happy?" he enquired, standing back at last.

"No, I'm not!" gasped Paddington, struggling to a sitting position. "I thought you were going to show me the ropes."

"The ropes? Ah!" Mr Constantine's face cleared as though a great misunderstanding had been resolved. "You do not want more pummels? You want other things . . . right?"

Paddington nodded frantically, glad that he'd made his point at long last.

"Come!" Mr Constantine lifted Paddington off the bed and then beckoned him through a doorway into the next room. "I will show you!"

Paddington had barely staggered a couple of paces when he felt himself being picked up again.

"Hooray!" shouted Mr Constantine, as he placed him onto a rope hanging from the ceiling and began pushing it to and fro. "Good for tummy, no?"

"No!" shouted Paddington, clinging on for dear life.

"Whoooopeeeeeee!" cried Mr Constantine, as he lifted Paddington off the rope and placed a belt round his middle. He pressed a switch. "Make you tingle, yes?"

"Yessssssss!" shuddered Paddington, as the belt began to vibrate.

If his experience on the couch had seemed like a bad dream his present situation was more like a nightmare. And as with a nightmare, so all sense of time vanished as he found himself being carried from one machine to the next.

"Phewwwww!" gasped Mr Constantine, as he lifted Paddington off some rollers and pushed him into a room full of steam. "Very hot. Good for pores!"

"Uhgggggg!" shivered Paddington shortly afterwards, as he clambered out of a pool of ice-cold water. As far as he could make out his paws were beyond help of any kind, for they felt as if they had long ago become detached from the rest of his body.

How long it lasted he had no idea, but when he at last crawled out into more normal surroundings he wasn't a bit surprised to discover it was already dark outside.

He sat in the middle of the corridor for quite some time, making sure he was still in one piece, until gradually he became aware that someone was addressing him.

"You can't stay there," said a lady in a white uniform. "Someone might trip over you."

She looked down at him sympathetically. "You'd better come along with me. I'll take you to the dining-room. I expect you could do with your evening meal."

Paddington picked himself up, a look of undying gratitude filling his face as he followed the lady along the corridor, all thoughts of detective work driven from his mind for the time being.

So far as he was concerned he'd solved the mystery of how Val, John and Peter had been robbed. He felt sure that if they'd spent only a quarter of the time he had with Mr Constantine they'd probably been in no fit state to resist any kind of attack.

"I should try and get a seat near the television," whispered the lady as she led Paddington into a large, table-filled room. "The Galloping Gourmet's on and he's most popular–especially with some of our long-term residents. If you like to make yourself at home I'll ask the waitress to bring you a spoon."

Raising his hat, Paddington thanked the lady very much and then collapsed into a chair, stretching his aching paws as he took in his new surroundings.

To say that the Galloping Gourmet was popular struck him as being the understatement of the year. He'd never seen such a crowd round a television set before. They were positively drooling over it.

Mr Kerr seemed to be having trouble with a cheese soufflé, part of which had fallen on the floor, but Paddington only gave him a fleeting glance. He had much more important things on his mind at that moment. Despite his ordeal a pleasant, warm glow had started to work its way up through his body, and already his taste buds were throbbing at the thought of the meal to come. A warm feeling of anticipation filled his mouth, for he particularly liked the sound of a restaurant where they didn't bother with the niceties of a knife and fork, and he sat up eagerly as a waitress bearing a silver tray entered the room and headed in his direction.

To his surprise, apart from a spoon and a bottle the tray was completely bare.

The spoon was a bit of a disappointment as well. He'd been hoping for something a good deal bigger. But he watched with interest as the lady opened the bottle and poured out a level measure of an orange-coloured liquid.

"There you are, dear," she said brightly, handing him the spoon. "Mind you don't spill any. I'm afraid they don't allow seconds."

"*Seconds!*" exclaimed Paddington hotly. "I haven't even had my firsts yet!"

"Ssh!" hissed a voice from the direction of the television set.

"Think yourself lucky you've got carrot juice," called someone else. "All *I've* had today is half a glass of hot water!"

"Don't eat it too fast," warned the waitress, picking up the tray as she turned to leave. "You don't want to get indigestion."

Paddington stared at the spoon in his paw as if he

could hardly believe his eyes. The way he felt at that moment indigestion was likely to be the least of his problems. He could have swallowed his meal, spoon and all, without it even touching the sides of his throat.

"Four pounds!" he exclaimed bitterly, addressing the world in general. "Four pounds for a pummel and a teaspoon of carrot juice!"

Slumping back in his chair he gazed mournfully round the dining-room. The trouble the Galloping Gourmet appeared to be having with his soufflé was nothing compared with the bother he was having with his stomach. He'd never been quite so hungry in all his life and he felt very glad he'd managed to keep his hat on throughout the proceedings.

Taking it off, he reached inside the lining and withdrew a small paper parcel which he carefully unwrapped.

Shortly afterwards a steady munching sound began to fill the air.

It was a sound that seemed to have a strange effect on the atmosphere in the dining-room. One out of all proportion to its size.

In fact, had the other occupants been included in any kind of survey, the Galloping Gourmet's view-

ing figures would have shown a sudden and most unexpected downwards swing at that moment, as one by one they turned their attention away from the television screen and concentrated it on Paddington.

A sob broke out from someone at the back of the crowd, and several of those nearest to him, unable to bear the strain a moment longer, rose to their feet and began advancing towards him with a most unholy gleam in their eyes, but fortunately for Paddington's digestive system he was much too busy enjoying himself by then to notice.

Paddington wasn't the sort of bear to be caught napping in an emergency. So far as he was concerned he was living through one of the biggest he'd ever experienced in the whole of his life, and he remained blissfully unaware that there was an even bigger one drawing closer every moment.

The receptionist looked at Paddington sternly.

"Eating marmalade sandwiches in our dining-room," he said, "is strictly forbidden."

He turned to the rest of the Browns gathered round his desk. "It's a good job you came when you did. I wouldn't have been responsible otherwise. Some of our residents were so upset they had to be put to bed early. We might well have had a riot on our hands."

"This isn't an ordinary sort of hotel, you know," he continued. "This is a health centre. People come here to lose weight–not to put it on."

Paddington listened with growing astonishment. He'd never heard of anyone wanting to lose weight before, let alone actually paying for the privilege.

"It doesn't sound very healthy to me," he exclaimed, giving the man a hard stare. "Besides, I *always* keep a marmalade sandwich under my hat."

"What I'd like to know," said Mr Brown, hastily changing the subject, "is why you came here in the first place?"

Paddington took a deep breath. So much had happened in such a short space of time he hardly knew what to say.

"It all started when I was late for a Blue Peter programme, Mr Brown," he began. "The one where Val, John and Peter were robbed."

"Robbed?" repeated Mr Brown. He turned to his wife. "I didn't hear anything about a robbery, did you, Mary?"

"Well," Mrs Brown looked at the others uneasily. "Paddington *did* mention it, but I'm afraid I was rather busy at the time and . . ."

Judy gave a sudden exclamation as light began to dawn at last. "But it wasn't pounds *money* they lost," she broke in. "It was pounds avoirdupois. We saw it while we were away."

"Pounds avoirdu*paws!*" exclaimed Paddington. He examined his own paws with interest. "No

wonder mine feel a bit funny."

Jonathan exchanged glances with his sister. "Judy means pounds weight," he explained patiently. "Val, John and Peter were so busy rehearsing on the machines all day they must have lost quite a bit."

"And judging by the state this young bear's in I'm not at all surprised," said Mrs Bird, fixing the receptionist with a gimlet eye.

"Not," she continued, turning back to Paddington, "that that's altogether a bad thing in some cases. Especially," she added meaningly, "as I happen to have prepared a particularly large dinner for tonight. I think we'd better pay the bill and leave the rest of the explanations until later. We don't want it to spoil."

Paddington pricked up his ears. Or rather he raised them as far as they would go in their present weakened condition, for Mrs Bird's words were the sweetest he'd heard for a long time.

In the circumstances he was quite happy to leave the explanations for as long as anyone liked.

"Perhaps," he said politely to the man behind the desk, "if I have an extra helping I may have to come back."

The receptionist gave a shudder, but before he had time to think up a suitable reply Paddington had disappeared.

Apart from looking forward to one of Mrs Bird's dinners he was anxious to get home as quickly as possible. Although there was still some time to go before the next Blue Peter programme he didn't want to run the risk of missing one ever again.

HARGREAVES

Tippoo's Tiger

Of all the spoils of war, Tippoo's Tiger must be just about the most peculiar! In the olden days, when conquering British soldiers sent home their treasures, the usual sort of thing that would turn up would be swords and guns and suits of armour. But one day, a crate was delivered to the Library of the famous East India Company. The Librarian opened the box, took a look inside, and with his quill pen made a neat note in his ledger:

"July 29th, 1808. Rec'd. Tippoo's Musical Tiger", and he put the Tiger on public exhibition. People were fascinated by it, and so was I when I saw it for the first time! I couldn't help laughing, because Tippoo's Tiger is a funny-looking beast, and when you turn a handle, it roars and groans! But it's a grisly joke, because the wooden Tiger's mauling an Englishman, and at every turn he waves his arm in despair.

If you stop and think, there's really nothing funny in a man having his head chewed off, but for Tippoo Sultan, it was the best joke in the world, and the Tiger was specially made to delight him.

Tippoo Sultan had two great passions in his life. One was for tigers, which he admired and respected above all other creatures–and one was for Englishmen, whom he loathed and despised as much as he loved tigers.

His very name "Tippoo" meant Tiger, and he tried to live up to all the tiger-like qualities he admired the most. He was fierce and cunning, his clothes were bright and beautiful like the tiger's fur, and in the same way that the tiger is lord and master of the jungle, Tippoo Sultan was all-powerful in his kingdom.

When he was a boy, he fought in his father's army against the British soldiers who had come to conquer India–and his father's army lost. From that moment on, Tippoo hated the English, and everything to do with them. When he grew up and became Sultan in his own right, he was absolutely determined that any Englishman who dared to set foot inside his territory should be thrown into a dungeon or killed with dreadful cruelty. It wasn't just that he hated men with white faces, for at his court were Frenchmen, and the Emperor Napoleon himself was his friend and ally.

So for many years, Tippoo ruled his kingdom of Seringapatum sitting on a tiger-shaped throne decorated with ten small tiger heads made of gold with shining jewels for eyes. As he lolled back in his throne, over his head was a canopy decorated with tiger stripes of real, glittering gold, fringed with beautiful pearls, and on either side of him stood the stone-faced soldiers of the royal guard, each man dressed in a special tiger-striped uniform. Tippoo himself wore tiger-striped jackets and turbans, and he blew his nose on a tiger-striped handkerchief.

One day, news reached Tippoo's court that a young Englishman called Mr Munro had been pounced on by a tiger, dragged off into the jungle and chewed to bits. When Tippoo heard the story, he laughed, for this poor young man was the son of his great enemy, Sir Hector Munro, who had defeated his father's army. To please the Sultan, the craftsmen at his court built a big, wooden tiger, painted it in brilliant stripes, carved an Englishman and shoved him in its mouth! Then, one of the French engineers made a musical organ that growled and built that into the tiger, too!

Tippoo was delighted! He turned the handle hour after hour, and the growling, wheezing, musical tiger never failed to amuse him.

But Tippoo's end was near. He woke one morning to find the British army at the gates of his city.

Batteries of cannon blew the stone walls to bits and soon the kingdom of Seringapatum was overrun by British soldiers. Tippoo fought like a tiger, but at the end of the day, he was found dead–a sword still in his hand!

So the British became masters of his kingdom and Tippoo's treasures were sent back to England. A golden tiger from his throne was sent to King George III as a present. The tiger-shaped cannons of Tippoo's army were packed up too. So were the carpets from his palace, and Tippoo's striped war jacket and turban, which were given as presents to famous men in England. And Tippoo's musical tiger was sent back to become a public show-piece. You can see it to this day if you visit the Victoria and Albert Museum in London.

Nobody much remembers now the awful tale behind it. Today the Musical Tiger is just a joke for everybody, just as it once was for Tippoo, the Tiger Sultan of Seringapatum.

Kathakali!

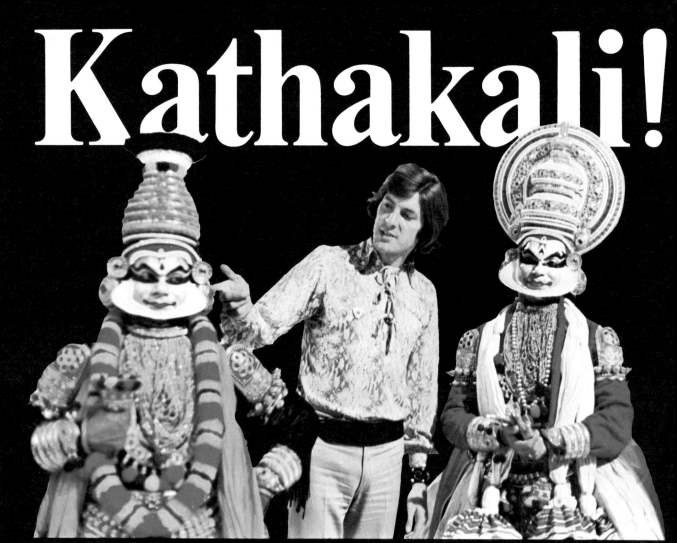

Imagine getting ready to take part in a play and spending seven hours putting on your make-up! It takes us about fifteen minutes to make up for the Blue Peter colour cameras, and the time John dressed up as Henry VIII, he spent two hours being turned into a plump, bearded king–but a whole seven hours' preparation is part of the normal routine for the famous Kathakali dancers from Kerala in India, and when you look at these pictures, you'll be in no doubt as to why they take so long.

Good characters always have their faces painted green.

Evil characters have knife patterns on both cheeks.

A wicked character with red beard and furry arms.

Kathakali means "dance story" and to help them tell their stories, the dancers put the most elaborate make-up on their faces, which makes it look as though they're wearing masks. Each kind of character in every story has a special make-up. For instance, good characters like heroes and gods have their whole face painted green—apart from their lips and eyebrows. Evil characters have fiery-red knife patterns drawn on both cheeks and savage white nose knobs. And the most wicked characters of all have red beards, black faces and white moustaches, and their furry costumes show they are like wild beasts.

A lot of the characters have face frames which stick out and give a mask-like, 3-D effect. They are made of thin rice paper so they're not at all heavy, and the paper's built up in layers stuck together with rice paste.

The dancers have special make-up artists who travel everywhere with them and who build up the masks, cutting out the sheets of rice paper to the right shapes and glueing them on, and they supervise the whole of the make-up operation. To become an expert in Kathakali make-up, you begin your training when you're about 8 years old, and it's just as hard work as the actual dancing.

The dancers train when they're aged 8, too, and it's a very tough job indeed. Altogether, it takes ten years to learn all the steps, and the boys have to be massaged every day between 4 o'clock and 7 o'clock in the morning, to make their muscles supple, which is dreadfully painful. So much so that in olden times, there was a rule that a boy was only accepted for training on condition that his parents didn't visit the school for a year, in case they were upset by hearing his screams as he was being massaged—by his trainer's feet!

When the Kathakali Company visited the Blue Peter studio, we

The dancers themselves paint the elaborate patterns on their faces, but it's quite impossible for them to complete their make-up unaided.

One of the team of make-up artistes who shape and fix the complicated face frames. Learning to become an expert in Kathakali make-up is just as hard as learning to become a dancer.

67

were just as fascinated by their costumes as by their make-up. All the dancers wore very full skirts and the fullness came from putting a kind of crinoline over a tutu, or stiff skirt, like ballet dancers sometimes wear.

Then came no less than five jackets, which seemed to be impossibly hot, until we discovered the dancers had their own built-in cooling system—each of the jackets was split down the back, so that in between dances they could be fanned with some welcome cool air. It takes many months to make each costume, and the enormous head-dresses, too. Some of the head-dresses

were two feet high—rainbow-coloured, with gold and semi-precious jewels and sparkling embroidery. And the dancers' hands sparkled, too—because fixed to their nails they wore curved, silver, false ones. All the dancers wore bells on their legs—not on their ankles, but tied below their knees, and these were very important because they helped to emphasise the rhythm of their steps.

Although we couldn't actually *talk* to the dancers—they didn't speak English, and we knew no Malayalam, we were beginning to admire them very much indeed. And then we discovered some-

thing else they did superbly well. Because the Kathakali dances tell such complicated stories, the dancers have to be experts in mime. They are able to twist and move their faces just as they twist their feet and bodies when they dance—and even a small flicker of an eyebrow has a meaning. There are special face movements to show things like love and fear, laughter and disgust, sadness and hatred. And one dancer called Guru Chathunni Panicker gave a magnificent performance of something called the Lotus Movement. We were told he was going to be a man watching a bee flying into a lotus flower. His

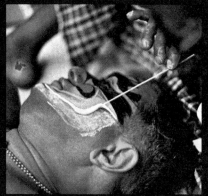

Rice paste is used as glue to stick on the face frames.

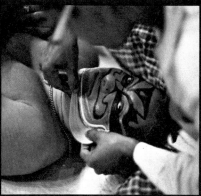

Very carefully, the face frame is stuck on in layers.

The frames can be all shapes and sizes.

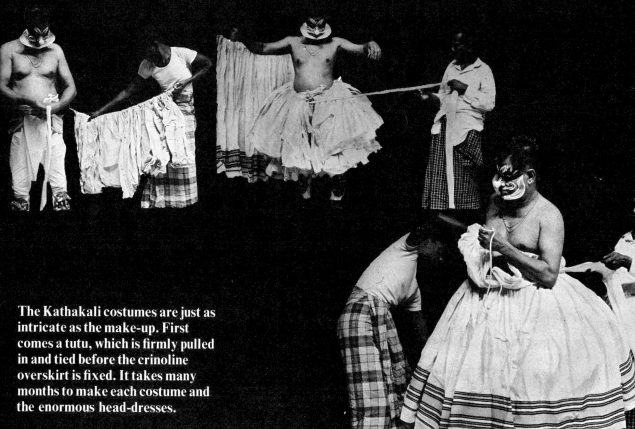

The Kathakali costumes are just as intricate as the make-up. First comes a tutu, which is firmly pulled in and tied before the crinoline overskirt is fixed. It takes many months to make each costume and the enormous head-dresses.

hands were the flower—that we could understand—but we just couldn't imagine how he could act the bee at the same time. But we'd forgotten Guru Chathunni Panicker's eyes! They seemed to swivel round his face on stalks as they watched the imaginary bee gathering pollen. In the end, we were totally convinced we'd all seen the bee—which proves how effective really good miming is!

You might be thinking that all these preparations for one performance are a bit of a waste of time. But with Kathakali dancing, a performance doesn't last one or two hours, it lasts the whole night through—in the open air—until the dancers are so exhausted they fall to the ground.

This had us worried for a bit. What would happen if they wouldn't stop and danced all through the 6 o'clock news? But all was well. Somehow the dancers got the message, in spite of the language difficulties, and managed to present a special performance of their three-hour Chariot Dance in under three minutes.

With our studio lights turned low, the rhythmic drumming and tinkling of hundreds of tiny bells, the dancers didn't seem like human beings. The magic of their make-up and costumes really had transformed them into gods, heroes and demons—for a few moments we completely forgot we were in the middle of the Blue Peter studio at Shepherd's Bush in London—which is just about the biggest compliment you can pay any actors or dancers anywhere in the world!

After seven hours the make-up is complete and the Chariot Dance can begin. Here two villains have captured the "heroine" who is, in fact, a man! Traditionally, in Kathakali dancing all female parts are played by men. Their faces are painted a flesh colour which is supposed to represent the feminine soul.

tap dancing

A few years ago, I watched some old Fred Astaire pictures on television. They looked a bit old-fashioned compared with today's films, but there's no getting away from it, Fred was a fantastic dancer. Watching him, I thought how marvellous it would be to be able to leap from table to table in top hat, white tie and tails, without getting one hair out of place or missing a single beat of music. Fred made it look so easy that I thought I'd find out a bit about tap dancing, so one day last Spring, full of optimism, I went to the Bush Davies School to join a class for my first lesson.

Rachel, one of the young students, was waiting to meet me with a pair of tap shoes in her hand.

"Good-morning, John," she said. "These are your tap shoes. When you've put them on, will you come over and join the class."

I'd never worn tap shoes before—they've got thick metal plates fixed on to the soles and heels, and they make a very satisfactory clattering noise as you walk across the floor.

Mrs. Meyer started the class as I took my place.

"As John's just joined us, we'll start with a simple warming up exercise—spring, hop, spring, hop, spring, spring, spring and—1—2—3—4—5—6—7—8." Out of the corner of my eye, I watched Rachel and I followed her as best I could. Actually

it wasn't very difficult and I began to think that top hat and white tie and tails weren't all that far away.

But I met my Waterloo with the time step. The time step is the real key to tap dancing. It's got to be as automatic as riding a bike, and believe me, it's twice as difficult. Still Fred Astaire had to learn the time step once, so with Rachel to help me, I stuck at it until I could *nearly* do it in slow motion.

I must admit, I was near to despair, when Patrick Harvey, the pianist who had been sympathetically watching me suffer, suddenly struck up with "Barnacle Bill", our Blue Peter signature tune, played in time to my dancing. If we played

70

it at that speed on the programme, it would be time to say "we'll be back on Thursday," before we said "Hello There"! But it did something for me. Maybe it was like the old war horse hearing the bugle call to charge. No matter, with some determination and a lot of help from my friend, Rachel, and teacher, Mrs. Meyer, I'd just about mastered it by the end of the lesson.

Right next door to the school there's a theatre, and Mrs. Meyer and the girls had arranged a special show so that I could put what I had learned into practice, before an audience. The audience consisted of the rest of the girls from the school, but that wasn't really a comfort, because I would be dancing before some of the most critical eyes in Britain.

There was to be a chorus of eleven girls and a co-star. No, they hadn't flown Fred Astaire from Hollywood, but they'd done almost as well. My old friend, Roy Castle, is a marvellous dancer, and he very kindly came along to do a solo spot—and a duet with me.

The audience was in—the house lights were fading—and Roy and I were standing in the wings ready to make an entrance.

The stage manager gave us a thumbs up and a reassuring grin as she said with portentous calm "Stand by—electrics; Stand by—sound; Stand by—curtain; Ladies and gentlemen, this is your one-minute call."

The orchestra struck up the opening bars of "We're a couple of swells" and I had bigger butterflies in my tummy than I've ever had before on Blue Peter.

"Good luck, John. Are you nervous?" asked Roy.

"A bit," I answered, "Are you?"

"Not really," he replied. "Let's have a look at that step again." Obediently, and rather haltingly, I went through my famous time step.

"Now I *am* nervous," said Roy. "Come on, you're on!"

The music rose to a crescendo, and Roy and I made an entry in front of the girls. It was carefully

I joined the class, and straight away, I was told to put on a pair of tap shoes

I laced up my shoes and started with a warming up exercise. This wasn't very difficult but.....

I met my Waterloo with the *time step*. It's the real key to tap dancing and it must be completely automatic

arranged for Roy to have all the difficult steps, but he made all the tricky stuff seem a great deal easier than my time step!

After a spot from the girls, Roy, with a great big grin on his face, went into a brilliant solo. And then it was my turn. I listened carefully to the music for my cue—took a deep breath—and somehow or other, I was in the spotlight, and—to my eternal amazement—doing more or less the right steps.

I don't think Fred Astaire needs to come out of retirement to face the challenge of a great new tap dancer from Halifax. But thanks to Roy and the girls, I'd thoroughly enjoyed myself, and I'd learnt that something else wasn't nearly so easy as it looks when it's performed by the experts!

At the theatre, with my friend Roy Castle, I performed before an audience of girls from the school. With Roy's terrific performance, the show was a complete success!

A Case of Double Treachery

It was the most luxurious plane that Bob had ever seen. The standard of Abbabiddi was flying over the cockpit of the VC-10 and inside the aircraft the Sultan himself was relaxing before his important mission.

Bob's uncle, Detective Sergeant McCann, had been seconded from Scotland Yard on a special duty. He was personal bodyguard to His Imperial Majesty the Sultan of Abbabiddi while he had been paying a state visit to the Queen. Now he was flying to the Island of Malta, G.C., to sign a vital international oil treaty, and Sergeant McCann was flying with him. For the young Sultan, lying back in his luxurious seat, it was a mission of great importance. For the good of the people of Abbabiddi he had decided, in spite of heavy opposition, to sign away his personal rights to the oil fields, and not only that, he had decided to abandon for ever his age-old custom of granting rich oil-bearing lands to the nobles of his country.

Bob was delighted to be allowed to travel on such an important flight. His uncle had been the Sultan's bodyguard all through the state visit that had taken place in London, and during that time the two men had become friends.

"Come to my country for a holiday," said the Sultan to McCann one day, "and bring your young nephew. A ride on a camel and a visit to the oil-wells would be interesting for him–and you, my friend, are always welcome at my palace. We shall be one day in Malta, and then your work will be done."

When Bob heard about the offer, he jumped at the chance, and now here he was, 35,000 feet above the Mediterranean, sharing coffee with a Sultan. To Bob it was like a dream!

"Sugar, your Imperial Majesty?" asked Bob.

"No thank you," said the Sultan. "Unlike most of my countrymen, I never touch it. I try to keep in training, so I have to watch my weight."

"Oh yes," said Bob. "I've seen you play tennis at Wimbledon. If you hadn't been a Sultan, would you have liked to be a professional tennis player?"

"I've often wondered," replied the Sultan. "Being left-handed has tremendous advantages, but I'm also very interested in flying. Perhaps I would like to have been a pilot."

"His Imperial Majesty would have been an international tennis player if he had so chosen," breathed El Grundi, the Sultan's sinister-looking aide. "But when this treaty is signed, he will be

famous for ever as a benefactor to the people of Abbabiddi."

"Don't forget that you, too, will be giving up some of your land," interrupted the Sultan.

"That is as your Majesty pleases," smiled El Grundi. "Where the eagle leads, the sparrow follows. Your wish is my command. And now, your Imperial Majesty, do you not wish to visit the flight-deck?"

"Yes," replied the Sultan. "I might even have a go at the controls. It will be quite a change after my own light aircraft."

Detective Sergeant McCann was about to follow the Sultan when El Grundi barred the way. "It will not be necessary for you to accompany His Majesty," he grunted. "There is no danger here, and there is very little room on the flight-deck," and he swept down the aisle following the Sultan.

"That didn't sound very friendly," said Bob, but his uncle just grinned and looked at the Mediterranean far below.

Half an hour later, the Sultan and El Grundi returned. Bob and Sergeant McCann rose as the two men sat back in their seats.

"Did you enjoy flying the aircraft, sir?" asked Bob.

"Yes," said the Sultan. "Those engines are remarkable. I've never flown at twice the speed of sound before! After all that excitement, I think I'd like a cup of coffee."

"Steward," cried El Grundi, "a cup of coffee for His Majesty!"

"With four lumps of sugar if you please," added the Sultan, and settled back in his chair.

Bob thought this might be a tactful moment and brought out his autograph book from his back pocket. "I wonder if your Imperial Majesty would honour me by signing my autograph book?"

"Certainly, my son," he responded, and taking out his solid gold pen with his right hand, he neatly wrote his name in Arabic characters.

Bob was delighted! "I've been trying to pluck up courage to ask for your signature ever since I saw you win at Wimbledon against Bev Taverstock."

"You saw that, did you?" said the Sultan. "He's a cunning player, and when he had me at 50 love, I thought the game was in his pocket."

"But you won in the end, didn't you?" laughed Bob.

"Yes," said the Sultan, "and I had the honour of receiving the trophy from the hand of my great friend, the heir to the Throne of England, His Excellency the Prince of Wales."

"His Imperial Majesty is tired now, McCann," broke in El Grundi. "I suggest that you and your nephew retire and leave us for a moment."

"Not just for a moment," answered Detective Sergeant McCann–his manner changing as he produced a revolver from his inside pocket.

"Both of you stay where you are!"

Bob was horrified. "Uncle!" he gasped. "What's the matter? I thought you were guarding His Majesty!"

"So I am," rasped McCann, "but this man's an impostor. If I'm not much mistaken, you'll find His Majesty a prisoner."

Bob dashed towards the cabin, and as he flung open the door, he heard a groan. There, lying on the bunk and hidden with a blanket, lay the Sultan, his hands and feet firmly bound. Taking out his pocket-knife, he quickly cut him free.

Seconds later, Bob returned with the real Sultan, and when he saw the man staring down at McCann's revolver barrel he could scarcely believe his eyes! The man was his double!

"It's like looking in a mirror," gasped the Sultan.

Bob was amazed. "They're exactly alike," he said. "Why has this happened? I don't understand!"

"I'll tell you why, you meddling English pig," snarled El Grundi. "His Imperial Majesty expected me to give away the lands that I have owned for years. I was determined that the foolish treaty should not be signed, and I intended to 'dispose' of His Majesty before we ever reached Malta."

"But he needed someone to stop the treaty," explained McCann, "so he found this evil man to pose as the Sultan. And he'd have got away with it, too, for I only spotted there was something up when he made five very careless mistakes."

"What were they?" queried Bob. "I didn't notice anything."

"I'll give you a hint," laughed McCann as he covered the villains with his gun. "You always land in trouble when the left hand doesn't know what the right is doing."

Did you spot the five clues? Turn to page 76 to check your answers.

Answers

Puzzle Pictures

1 A **slit gong** from the New Hebrides sent by Chief Tofur as a present to the Queen. The gong is now on display at University Museum, Cambridge.

2 This **Vickers Supermarine Spitfire** was brought to the Blue Peter studio by a member of 71 Mechanised Unit, RAF Bicester. The Spitfire is 29 feet 11 inches long and has a wing span of 36 feet ten inches.

3 A **double-ended Mini**–probably the only car in the whole of the world that can be driven from either end.

4 Combined with a bank of six tape recorders, the **VCS 3**–or **Voltage Controlled Studio**–can make hundreds of different sounds at the flick of a switch.

5 Two visitors from India. **The slender loris** is a nocturnal creature, sleeping by day and coming out at night to find its food.

6 Mr. Dolling's man-powered **flying machine.**

7 The latest thing in **chairs**–a set of giant dentures. The 32 teeth are made from padded PVC.

8 Yukon **Bud Fisher** pans for gold in the Blue Peter studio.

9 1900 and 1970 football clothes– and a selection of silver cups and trophies from the **World Football Exhibition.**

10 Strongman, **Walter Cornelius,** practises walking for charity on this giant tyre.

A Case of Double Treachery

1 The real Sultan said that he never took sugar in his coffee, but later the impostor called for four lumps!

2 The real Sultan was a famous tennis player, but the impostor didn't even know how to score (there's no such score as 50 love.)

3 The real Sultan said he was left-handed, but the impostor signed Bob's autograph book with his right hand.

4 The impostor said he flew the VC 10 at twice the speed of sound, but the real Sultan who was an experienced pilot would have known this was absolutely impossible.

5 The impostor referred to the Prince of Wales as His Excellency. If he had been on a State visit to London he would have known that the Prince of Wales is called His Royal Highness and not His Excellency. (And anyway, Prince Charles has never presented the trophies at Wimbledon.)

Biddy Baxter, Edward Barnes and Rosemary Gill would like to acknowledge the help of Gillian Farnsworth and Margaret Parnell

Designed by Haydon Young

All the photographs in this book were taken by Charles E. Walls with the exception of the following: Princess Anne (page 4) by Keystone Press; Royal Safari (page 9) by Nicholas Acraman; Blue Peter engine (lead picture, page 14) by Michael Cook; engine on side by the Daily Express; Blue Peter engine (foot of page 15) by British Rail (Eastern Region); Juan de Parejo (page 16) by Christie's; Las Maninas (page 17) by Giraudon Photographie; Photograph of John (foot of page 30) by Nigel Chmielowski; Gustave Eiffel (page 48) by Radio Times Hulton Picture Library; Paris view (page 50) by J. Allan Cash Worldwide Photographic Library; Picture postcard (page 54) by Camera Press; Tippoo (page 64) by permission of the Victoria & Albert Museum.

The Painter's Assistant was written by Dorothy Smith; Aztecs and Marie Antoinette were illustrated by Robert Broomfield, who also drew the soldier on horseback, page 49 and Tippoo, page 65. Bleep and Booster, Bengo cartoons, and Mystery Picture by . "Tim"; A Case of Double Treachery was illustrated by Bernard Blatch; Inside the 1903 Cadillac by Geoffrey Wheeler.

The cutting on page 57 is reproduced from the Brighton Evening Argus.

Useful Information

Blue Peter Locomotive Society, 116 Holgate Road, York. Y02 4BB.

Montagu Motor Museum, Beaulieu, Hants.

Dolphins, Brighton Aquarium, Marine Parade, Brighton.

Tippoo's Tiger is at the Victoria and Albert Museum, South Kensington, London S.W.7.

University Museum, Museum of Archaeology and Ethnology, Downing Street, Cambridge. Open: 2.00–4.00 p.m.

Guinness Book of Records, 2 Cecil Court, London Road, Enfield, Middlesex.

How to win a "Blue Peter" badge: By sending us interesting letters, good ideas for the programme, drawings, paintings, and models that have been particularly well made–and we award competition badges, too.

"Blue Peter" Mini books: Book of Television Book of Teddy's Clothes Book of Pets Safari to Morocco Expedition to Ceylon Book of Presents Book of Daniel Book of Guide Dogs Blue Peter Royal Safari

Royal National Lifeboat Institution, 42 Grosvenor Gardens, London S.W.1.

Our Blue Peter Lifeboats are stationed at:

Blue Peter I	:	Littlehampton (Tel. 3922)
Blue Peter II	:	Beaumaris (Tel. 589)
Blue Peter III	:	North Berwick (Tel. 2963)
Blue Peter IV	:	St. Agnes (Tel. 251)

If you are making a long journey to see one of the boats, it's best to telephone to make sure someone will be on duty. As all four stations are manned by volunteers, they are not open constantly each day.

Blue Peter Competition

Would you like to meet Valerie, John, Peter and the rest of the Blue Peter team? Would you like to see all the animals? Would you like to come to London and have tea with them all? This is your chance!

Look at these mystery words–

EESGAAODERNLGC
RNLEWREOLTIAUCS
XADNDIIOVN
CSRNAPEINENS
ARCEYTSOL
DWEHRESOPRAT
CAADRRBEHKIR
OOEYLCR
HYNJMPLANHOE
ORBNGSNKODA

They are all names of people who have been on Blue Peter during the last year– if you find some of them difficult, look carefully through the book for some clues! When you have deciphered the names, write them on a piece of paper like this (we've done the first one for you to show you what to do):

EESGAAODERNLGC–
George Cansdale

Carry on like this until you have a list of all the people.

The First Prize will be an invitation to an exciting

Blue Peter Party

and there will be lots of competition badges for the runners-up, too.

First Prize winners and runners-up will be notified by letter. The closing date for entries is 12th January 1972.

Send your answers together with your entry form to:

Blue Peter Competition,
BBC Television Centre,
London W12 7RJ.

77